her unexpected detour

a Checkerberry Inn novel

KYRA JACOBS

Entangled Publishing, LLC
2614 South Timberline Road
Suite 109
Fort Collins, CO 80525
Visit our website at www.entangledpublishing.com.

Bliss is an imprint of Entangled Publishing, LLC. For more information on our titles, visit http://www.entangledpublishing.com/category/bliss

Edited by Alycia Tornetta
Cover design by Heather Howland
Cover art from iStock

Manufactured in the United States of America

First Edition September 2015

Bliss
an Entangled imprint

To my mother, who taught me the joy of gardening at an early age.
I love you, Mom.

Chapter One

As Kayla Daniels slid into a booth at the EAT diner, she wondered how her week could have ended in such utter disaster. The image of her boss came to mind yet again, his brows furrowed and face a shade of red she hadn't known possible. How could he truly believe she intentionally sent that malicious email? She had lived and breathed everything Wayne Advertising the past four years, spent countless hours both on and off the clock, and what was her reward? A week off with no pay. So much for her spotless track record, or any hope of ever moving up in the company.

"Coffee?"

Kayla looked up to find a young waitress beside the table, notepad in hand and half apron tied tight around her hips. The woman's Barbie-like proportions, stylish pixie cut, and dyed autumn-red hair seemed out of place at the aging dive. A hypocritical thought, Kayla realized, as she didn't exactly fit in with the diner's clientele today, either. They were dressed in denim and flannel, she in silk and rayon.

"Um, yes. Please."

Pixie Cut popped her gum and walked off without another word. Yep, Kayla was overdressed. Maybe she should have stopped at home to change before coming up to see Tommy. Then again, this three-hour coffee run hadn't exactly been planned.

Oh, she'd fully intended to stay at work after receiving that royal reaming from Phillip Jacober. She had marched out of his office with her chin held high. Once she returned to her cramped cubicle, though, reality set in, and tears of betrayal had blurred her vision.

Which was ridiculous, she thought, as she worked like mad to keep them contained. Kayla was too much of a professional to have some silly breakdown over a tongue-lashing, deserved or not. All she needed was a little fresh air to clear her mind. So she'd hurried out, told the receptionist she was off to make a quick coffee run. But when the turn lane for Starbucks came into view, she kept right on driving.

Now, perched on a lumpy vinyl cushion three hours north of home, Kayla felt a twinge of guilt. She'd never bailed on work before. Then again, she'd never gotten suspended before, either. Apparently today was a day of firsts. Yet another reason to get the heck out of Dodge, before anything else in her life could go wrong.

She dragged in a deep, cleansing breath and pushed this morning's debacle from her mind. The aroma of artery-clogging comfort food was like a warm blanket to her soul and slowly began to calm her frayed nerves. EAT would never win an award for being the most pristine establishment, but the college-town eatery had something the chain restaurants never would: character. Well, that, and a permanent layer of grease coating its white linoleum-topped tables, chipped black and white tile floors, and probably even a few regular patrons planted along the bar top that ran the length of the building.

The rumble of a nearby engine drew her attention to the window beside her table. Outside, a large black Silverado pulled into the lot and parked. On its side was a logo that read MASTERSON CONTRACTING. Kayla watched as the driver pushed his door open and stepped out. He was a tall, dark, beefcake kind of guy, with steel-gray eyes that matched the rain-heavy clouds looming overhead.

Now there was a guy who wouldn't have taken a load of crap from his boss this morning. No sirree. That guy probably would have taken the suspension papers and shoved them where the sun don't shine.

If only I'd had the nerve to do the same.

Then again, doing something like that would have gotten her fired, not just suspended. How could she possibly expect to hide something like that from her father, especially since he and her boss were old college buddies? No, he'd find out soon enough, and then he'd start to worry. And the last thing she wanted was for him to start worrying again—he'd gone through far more of that with her mom's illness than anyone ever should.

Mr. No-Nonsense walked beyond her line of sight, and Kayla gave herself a mental slap. Enough beating herself up. What she needed was an ear to bend, a fresh perspective, and maybe even a little sympathy. She reached for her phone and tapped a familiar number, the motion nearly on autopilot. After three and a half rings, the deep, groggy voice of her brother Tommy came on the line.

"What?"

"Well, good morning to you, too," she said.

"Ugh, it's still morning?"

Kayla rolled her eyes. "If you can even call it that. It's eleven already. Are you seriously still in bed?"

"Yes, I am," he growled. "And you would be, too, if you'd stayed up until three working on a transmission for your buddy and didn't have a class until one."

"Yikes, sorry, I had no idea. Maybe I could make it up to you? Buy you lunch?"

"Lunch?"

Across the line, Tommy's mattress creaked. Kayla could picture him sitting up in bed holding the phone to his ear with one hand and rubbing his eyes with the other. Poor kid had never been a morning person. Working on cars until wee hours of the morning probably didn't help any.

"Yeah, sure. Whatever. Oh, wait—I've got plans this weekend. Could we try for n—"

"Not this weekend, Tommy. Today. As in, right now."

Tommy chuckled. "I appreciate your vote of confidence in my new engine, Kay, but the Prix can't get me to Fort Wayne that fast. Yet."

"It doesn't have to—I'm already in town. At EAT, second booth from the door on the right. "

The joking tone left his voice. "Okay, you're starting to freak me out. What's going on? You never miss work. Ever."

Day of firsts…

"Yeah, I know. I'll explain when you get here."

Brent Masterson eased into his customary seat at EAT's counter and nodded a hello to today's waitress. The redhead. Ten to one odds she'd screw up his order again. Where the hell was Marge lately, anyway?

Maybe she'd finally woken up, escaped Mount Pleasant, Michigan before this town sucked the life right out of her. It had a way of doing that with the rest of its locals, himself included.

"Mornin'," Red said as she filled his coffee mug. "The usual?"

"I don't know. You gonna get it right this time?"

The red-haired beauty whose legs seemed to go on forever narrowed her hazel eyes. "Two eggs over easy, three strips of bacon—slightly overcooked. Two links of sausage—mild not hot. And one piece of whole wheat toast with strawberry jam, not jelly, on the side. That sound about right?"

"Sure does. Thanks, darlin'," he said with a wink. The irritated look on her face faded to a blushing grin.

Yep, Brent thought as she walked away. He still had it. Too bad he was surrounded by college kids. Plenty of eye candy to go around, just not a whole lot of mental sustenance to go along with it. Not that he was scouting for a girlfriend.

He pulled the morning paper from his back pocket and skimmed the front page. Bank robbery. Casino expansion. Crappy economy. He sighed. Same shit, different day. At least the Tigers were on a three-game winning streak. He'd shove that in Miles's face later, the damn Yankees fan.

"Thanks, but I'll wait. I'm expecting someone."

Brent slid his hand into the handle of his mug and glanced in the direction of that unfamiliar silky voice. Sitting a few booths over was a cute, young brunette he'd not seen in here before. She stuck out like a sore thumb among the diner's other patrons with her corporate look and manicured nails. Her gaze was trained on the parking lot, an expectant look on her pretty face.

No way he would have missed her before. A new professor at the college, maybe? Business traveler?

From down the bar, a cell phone burst out with "It's Raining Men." Brent turned to watch an acne-riddled co-ed scramble to silence her cell. *Kids these days,* he thought with a scowl. Everything was video games and smart phones, apps and tablets. He'd been able to keep up on technology while in college, but that was nearly a decade ago. A lot had changed since then. *He* had changed.

And the world had gone on without him.

Brent turned his attention back to the sports section, skimmed through the recap of yesterday's Tiger's game stats, then flipped to the paper's editorial section. Sure enough, there it was, just like Ruby had said on the phone this morning—a column at the top of the page, written by the paper's own chief editor, weighing the possible impact of a big name box store coming to Mount Pleasant. And damn if they didn't list a whole lot more positives than negatives.

He wondered who paid the Tribune off to publish that load of garbage, because no one around here would ever think about selling their land to a bunch of money-hungry corporate leeches. Especially not his grandmother. Though, when Miles saw this, Brent knew his cousin would start pushing her again to let the inn go.

Brent's scowl deepened. Sure, the money would be great to have, and Ruby could finally take a worry-free plunge into retirement. But she wasn't ready to give up the inn, and he'd be damned if he was going to let anyone force her into it, least of all their own flesh and blood.

Frowning, he pushed off his barstool and started for the john. Only, something collided with him before he took a single step. Something smaller than him, and softer, and... smelling of flowers and vanilla?

"Oof!"

Instinctively, he reached out to catch the body rebounding off his chest. A curvy, feminine body, that just happened to belong to the cute brunette. He started to give her a quick once over, to make sure she hadn't been hurt upon impact. But his gaze stalled on her sexy black heels, lean athletic legs, and tight black skirt hugging a pair of slender hips. Her light purple, button-down blouse gapped open at the top due to the awkward angle he'd caught her, revealing a glimpse of her lacy, cream-colored bra.

"I'm so sorry!" she said. "I didn't realize you were..."

"Moving?" A pair of bright blue eyes snagged his attention. Brent swallowed hard. "Yeah, guess I forgot my turn signal. You all right?"

"I'm fine. Thank you." The hint of a grin tugged at her perfect pink lips.

"Good," he said with a nod. "Good."

Brent wanted to kick himself. He sounded like a complete idiot. When was the last time he'd gone and gotten tongue-tied at the sight of some silly woman?

He relaxed his grip, watched to make sure Legs wouldn't topple over again, then let go altogether and took a step back. Brent needed to put some space between him and that alluring scent. Away from the temptation. He'd always been a sucker for nice legs.

Her grin slipped away. "Oh, you have got to be kidding me."

Brent's gaze followed hers to each of the dirty handprints he'd left on the arms of her silky blouse. She brushed at the marks with one hand, her scowl deepening when the drywall dust refused to disappear.

"Sorry about that. Was just headed to wash up."

"It's...don't worry about it." She ducked her head a little, stepped around him, and continued toward the restroom. "If this day gets any worse..."

Brent blew out a sigh as he watched that tight little ass of hers saunter away. Damn, she was hot. But princess there had dismissed him in a blink, more worried about her shirt than anything else. Definitely not his type.

So why did it bother him that she'd walked away without a single glance back?

Forget it, he told himself as she disappeared into the ladies' room. *Forget her.* Women were trouble, every single one of them. The last thing he needed was to be distracted by some prissy out-of-towner, especially after that article in today's paper. He had enough trouble brewing as it was.

Chapter Two

When Kayla returned to her seat, she reached for her coffee mug, then snuck a peek at the wall of a man she'd collided with on her way to the restroom. The one whose handprints she'd spent the last five minutes scrubbing out of her blouse. Of course it had to be Mr. No-Nonsense she'd tangled with, who'd turned out to be much better looking than she expected when they were all up close and personal. And scarier looking. Definitely not the kind of guy who takes orders from a corporate grouch.

She grinned. Maybe he could give her a few lessons. But only if it didn't involve any more damage to her already limited work wardrobe. She barely had enough cash to cover her rent this month, let alone a trip to the mall.

The silverware on Kayla's table began to dance and rattle. She looked up to spy her brother's car pulling into the lot, its engine loud and proud. *As it should be*, she thought with sisterly pride. Tommy had spent years perfecting his 2006

Grand Prix GTP. Knowing him, it was still far from finished.

He parked and headed for EAT's door, dressed in his usual attire: grease-stained jeans and a T-shirt sporting some motor company advertisement, partially covered by an unbuttoned, untucked flannel shirt. Only, his flannel looked more wrinkled than usual, and Kayla couldn't help but worry that he wasn't getting enough sleep more often than just today.

No, Tommy was a big boy. He didn't need her mothering him any more than he'd ever needed their mother doing that for him. Kayla had always been the one who'd needed that. But the gauntlet had been passed to her, far too early. *Stupid cancer…*

Her brother stepped inside, spied Kayla, and smiled as he sauntered over to her booth. "Hey there, stranger." Tommy pecked a quick kiss on her cheek, then slid onto the bench seat opposite her.

"Thanks for coming. And sorry again for waking you up."

"Water under the bridge, Sis." He leaned forward, his gaze intense. "So, you gonna tell me what you're doing here when you should be at work?"

Kayla sighed. "Well, I didn't plan on playing hooky. But I got called into Jacober's office and—"

"TJ!"

Kayla jumped as her waitress materialized beside them, hands fisted on her hips. Seriously, the woman needed to wear a bell around her neck or something. And why was Pixie Cut suddenly giving her the evil eye?

"Hey, I didn't think you were working this morning." A broad grin washed over Tommy's face as he reached out and laced his fingers through the waitress's free hand. "Heather, this is my sister, Kayla, from back in Indiana. Kayla, this is Heather."

"Oh." The daggers in Heather's eyes dulled to butter knives. "Nice to meet you."

"Likewise."

Heather offered her a placating smile, then shifted her attention back to Tommy. "So yeah, I switched shifts with Marge since we made plans for this weekend."

A coy smile stretched across her face, and Kayla wondered what secret she was missing out on. Then again, judging by the color blossoming on her brother's cheeks, maybe she didn't want to know.

"Whatcha want, TJ? The usual?"

Tommy gave her a nod. "I think so. Kayla?"

"Um, I'd just like the oatmeal, please. And a fruit cup."

Heather looked at her like she was an alien, then jotted the order down and popped her gum. "Okay, great. I'll get that in for you two and be back to check on your coffee."

"Thanks, Heather."

Pixie Cut strutted off, and Kayla eyed her brother. "*TJ?*"

His gaze cut from the retreating Heather back to hers, pink returning to his cheeks. "Yeah, you know. Sounds more appealing to the ladies." He waggled his eyebrows.

"Since when do you care about the ladies?"

"Since now," he said, grinning like a lovesick fool. Heather swung back by with a cup of joe for him on her way to another table. Once she was gone, the playful look left his eyes. "Okay, let's try this again. Why aren't you at work?"

"Let's just say I got upset."

"Upset?" He reached over to snag a sugar packet from

the stash of condiments on the window side of their table. "About what?"

"About being handed a week off with no pay."

"*What?*" Heads turned in their direction. Tommy lowered his voice, but the rage remained in his tone. "Why the hell would they give you a week off? And with no pay? If anything they owe you a week off, all expenses paid."

"Trust me, I'm with you on that. But something blew up in our faces this morning, and Jacober thinks I'm behind all of it."

"Blew up? What happened, you accidentally miss a few typos in an ad or something? Put a logo in the wrong spot?"

Kayla offered him a weak smile. "I wish. 'Cause that I could handle. But this? This was the wrong file altogether. Someone took my team's ad and modified it to include an image of two dogs, um, making puppies. Only, the faces of our biggest client and his wife were superimposed over where the dogs' heads should be."

"Oh, nu-uh."

"Yep. Right there, big and bold, smack dab in the center. All the rest of the copy was correct, but who would bother to keep reading after seeing..." Kayla clamped her eyes shut and shook her head. It was going to take years for that image to fade from her memory. Years.

"So, who did it?" Tommy asked.

"I don't know. Someone with a serious bug up his you-know-what."

"But it doesn't make sense—why would Jacober pin this on you?"

Kayla grimaced. "Because. I was the one who sent the email."

Shock clouded Tommy's normal happy-go-lucky countenance. "You did *what*?"

"Keep your voice down," Kayla said, chancing a quick glance at the tables around them. "It's embarrassing enough as it is."

"Kay, what the hell were you thinking?"

"It wasn't like that, all right? Look, when I left yesterday the image looked fine. Better than fine. In fact, it was perfect. One of our best. Then I come in today and there's a typed note on my desk asking me to double-check a change made to the headline one last time before I forward the ad on to the client for their review. I was a bit miffed someone had gone in and made a change after we'd finalized it yesterday, but last minute changes happen sometimes.

"When I opened the file to proof the changes, it was saved at a view zoomed in to the title. It looked fine, so I didn't bother to zoom out and look at the rest of the ad." She shook her head when Tommy threw her an incredulous look. "You've got to understand, I looked it over 'one last time' at least twelve times yesterday. And no one's ever pranked me at work before. So I hit send and half an hour later I'm getting my butt handed to me on a silver platter. I've never seen Jacober so mad before. He said if my track record hadn't been so squeaky clean they would have fired me on the spot. As it is, the board of directors might still decide to do just that."

Tommy snorted. "They won't fire you. You do everything around there. Hell, they'd be lost without you."

Kayla couldn't argue with that. In fact, she'd had that very same thought several times on her way up here.

"Since Jacober doesn't seem out to get you, that means

someone else wants you gone. Question is: who would stand to gain the most if you got canned?"

Tommy had a way of seeing past the BS that tripped up other people. Like now, focusing on identifying the who and why, not chastising Kayla for her mistake. It was one of the things she loved most about her little brother, and the main reason she'd come here. It was that or run to her father, but she worked hard enough to keep him from worrying as it was.

"I have no idea. Even worse, our team's proposal for the huge Foellinger project is due in two weeks. No one would want me gone right now."

Would they?

No, Kayla decided after a moment, everyone on her team got along great. Sure, she'd met some resistance when Mr. Jacober originally named her a team leader—she'd only been with the company for two years. But any animosity they'd harbored evaporated after that first brutal bidding war for Prairie Farms. Her team had come out on top then, and countless times since.

"If that's the case, then maybe it was someone who sits nearby and saw you leave." Tommy's features darkened. "Someone who had something to gain by you being fired. Or you getting sidelined at the very least."

"You're probably right. But who?"

Someone on another team. A coworker who had everything to gain by pulling a stunt like this, and absolutely nothing to lose—one of the perks of being the owner's stepson. Kayla's narrowed gaze met Tommy's as they spoke the now obvious answer in unison.

"*Joe Freimann.*"

"If I ever get my hands on that bastard..." Tommy's hands balled into fists. "And after all the times you've bailed out his sorry ass for missed deadlines and crappy work."

"Yeah. Really paid off, didn't it?"

Kayla had complained about Joe to her brother before. What she'd left out of those conversations, though, were all the times she'd also deflected Joe's romantic advances. Over, and over, and over. Maybe if she'd just caved in and gone on a date with the slimeball none of this would ever have happened?

Doubtful. Joe had a heart of stone and didn't care who he stepped on so long as he came out on top. He alone had transformed their office culture from a group of highly enthusiastic go-getters into a herd of downtrodden Eeyores. And all while her boss sat back and looked the other way.

This time, though, Joe had made a serious mistake: he'd singled out the only employee his stepdad couldn't feasibly fire. And if Joe thought she'd go down without a fight, well, he had another thing coming.

Thomas Granville set two cans of exterior, oil-based paint down on the counter with a grunt. "I hear there's a nasty storm moving in."

Brent cast a glance out the front window of Granville Supplies. "Yeah, well, I hope the weatherman's wrong. I hate freezing rain." He turned back and smirked at the aging widower. "Too bad you've got such a long hike home."

Tom waved him off with a snort. Not many people knew the brick, two-story shop tucked neatly away in the historic part of town doubled as his abode. Brent could still remember trips upstairs with his late grandfather. He and Miles would drink lemonade and play checkers while the older men exchanged war stories.

It felt like a lifetime ago.

"You sure these are what you want, Brent?" Tom said, gesturing toward the paint.

"Yeah, I'm sure."

The Checkerberry's monster porch was in dire need of a paint job. Miles had done his damnedest to talk Brent out of buying the high-end stuff, but he'd stood his ground. He knew from experience that the rumors about cheaper paints only lasting half as long as the expensive brands were all too true. Since he hated painting, the less often he had to repaint anything the better.

With a shrug, Tom turned and pulled two more cans of base color off a nearby shelf. "How's your grandmother?"

"Fine. She's fine."

"Glad to hear. And glad to see she's set to open the Checkerberry again in a few weeks. Was worried this weak economy might force her to close permanently."

"Oh, the inn's not out of the woods yet. She had half the customers we usually do last season, Tom. Half. Enough to stay in the black, but not by much. This year's gotta be better, or..." Brent shook his head. "It'd kill her to lose that place."

He felt a stab of guilt as Tom pried the lid off the first can. Maybe Brent should have gone with the cheaper paint. What if the inn didn't do better this summer? Or the next? This was her savings he was spending here.

Maybe Miles was right. Maybe she really should think

about selling the inn. Get out of the bed-and-breakfast in-dustry altogether, so she could move into one of those little retirement communities.

He couldn't help but smirk at that thought. Ruby would go stir-crazy in a place like that her first day there. Hell, her first *hour* there. No, buying this grade of paint was the right thing to do. He would make the Checkerberry shine like new and pray his grandmother's guests would somehow find their way back. They had to.

"Oh, Ruby's a tough old bird." Tom's face softened as he set the paint beneath the color dispenser. "I'm sure she'll be fine. Plus, she's got you and Miles to look out for her. And a dedicated staff."

Brent shook his head. "*Had* a dedicated staff. Her chef is on the fence about whether or not to return this season, and our groundskeeper turned in his resignation last month. Ruby just can't afford to pay them what they'd be making at the casinos in town."

"Now that's a stroke of bad luck. Has she found a new groundskeeper?"

"You're looking at him."

Tom gave him a fatherly frown. "What about your business, Brent?"

"Things were slow, anyway," he lied. "And who can tell Ruby no?"

Tom chuckled as he replaced the paint can's lid and moved the pail over to his well-worn mixer.

The machine jerked to life, and Brent's collision with the hot little brunette in the diner sprang to mind. All soft, curvy, and completely wrong for him.

He was a local, and she was anything but.

If Legs was smart, she'd get back on the road and leave this godforsaken town in her rearview mirror before it tried to sink its claws into her, too.

"Things will work out, son," Tom said. "'Round here, they always do."

Brent answered with a grunt.

Maybe for Tom that'd been true. But for Brent? Not so much.

Chapter Three

As she stepped from her car and struggled to find solid footing, Kayla took a quick scan of her frozen surroundings. One minute it'd been plain old rain falling from the sky, the next a curtain of ice. Bolting from Indiana before checking the forecast hadn't been a very wise decision on her part. Neither had been her assuming Tommy would let her stay over tonight.

Her second terrible assumption of the day.

But really, what were the chances of his roommate having a terrible case of the flu at the same time as her visit? She couldn't blame Tommy for planning a weekend trip over to Windsor with Heather to get away from the germs, but it'd killed Kayla's plans to crash there for the night.

Okay, so maybe crash wasn't the best choice of words right now. Not after her Impala had hit that slick spot in the middle of the intersection, slid into the ditch, and then ate a fence post. Between the ice now coating her windshield and that stupid construction detour, she'd somehow missed her turn to get back onto Business 127. Now she was stuck out here, in the middle of nowhere. In high heels. With zero bars on her cell phone.

Why did it feel like the whole world had it in for her today?

She half crawled, half scrambled up and out of the side ditch and squinted through the rain of ice pellets, looking for a passing motorist to flag down. But there were no cars in sight. Apparently, she was the only idiot on the road right now. Or at least, she *had* been.

Kayla hitched her purse higher onto her shoulder, eeny-meeny-miny-moed, and then stepped off in the winning direction to search for a house with a functional landline. Hopefully she'd find one before she slipped and broke her neck. Though with the way her day had gone so far, it wouldn't surprise her if that happened, too.

This run of bad luck can stop any time now…

Normally, the trip between Granville's Hardware and the Checkerberry Inn took Brent all of seven minutes. Eight, if one of Mr. Billings's alpacas got loose and wandered out onto the road again. But today's late spring storm had slowed his travels to an annoying crawl. Everything as far as the eye could see was slowly being suffocated by a layer of ice. Salt might have kept the roads from freezing, but unfortunately any of it left on the roads from last winter had been washed away by last week's rainy deluge.

Typical spring weather in Michigan.

The irritation coursing through Brent's veins intensified when he spotted a car up ahead that had slid off the road into the shallow ditch and taken out one of Ruby's neighbor's fence posts.

"Aw, come on. I just fixed that damned post last week!"

What was it with the people around here lately? That was the third time this year the post had been hit. *Maybe it's time to find a really big rock to set between it and the road...*

He hated the thought of being delayed any further, but whether the other driver was an idiot or not, Brent couldn't turn a blind eye to the situation. A quick glance, to make sure they were okay, he conceded. Maybe even an offer to call a tow truck. Nothing more. But as he pulled up alongside the ditch, he could see the car was empty, its driver already gone.

"Good," he muttered, and eased his truck forward once more.

His relief was short-lived. A few hundred yards ahead, he spotted a figure slip-sliding along the side of the road. A small, curvy figure, dressed in a jacket, skirt, and heels.

Heels? Who the hell walks around in the middle of an ice storm wearing heels?

At the sound of his approaching truck the figure turned and waved frantically in his direction. The sudden movement compromised her footing, and Brent watched with mild amusement as she did darn near everything *but* fall while struggling to stay upright. Balance recovered, she turned her face back toward his halting truck and threw him a sheepish grin.

Oh, no.

Brent rubbed his eyes.

Not her. Please God, anyone but her.

He blinked and looked again, but the view didn't change. It was Legs, her soaking wet clothes molded to every one of her mouth-watering curves. Temptation incarnate.

He gave serious thought to hitting the gas, just tearing out of there and never looking back. But that lasted all of half a second before the gentleman in him—the glutton-for-punishment gentleman—decided to do the right thing and help her out. With a silent vow to not get tongue-tied around her again, he drew his truck to a stop and lowered the passenger window.

"Let me guess," he called. "Decided to walk off some of that lunch?"

"Good guess, but no."

She brushed a clump of wet hair from her eyes, and those unassuming blues of hers managed to rattle something in him yet again. If she stuck around any longer, he'd have to stop making eye contact with her. Or, better yet, he thought as she stepped closer, maybe he should make sure she didn't stick around at all.

"Actually," she said, leaning her elbows on his truck's lowered window, "my car went off the road a ways back. And my cell can't seem to find a signal out here. Do you have a phone I could borrow?"

Ah, see? She'd make a call and be gone. It was a win-win all around. "Sure. Climb in."

Brent shifted in his seat and reached to dig the phone from his front pocket. Legs lowered her arms and took a small step back. He cast her a dark look. What, was his truck not good enough for her? "What's the matter?"

"Nothing." She hugged herself, glanced up and down the street. "Just…waiting for you to get your phone."

She didn't trust him. Though, being female, stranded, and looking the way she did, he couldn't really blame her. Still, he wasn't going to let her stand there and freeze to death. He retrieved his phone and held it out toward her.

Legs didn't budge.

A princess and stubborn—lucky me.

"Look, I'd feel a heck of a lot better if you'd come in out of the rain while you make your call. My phone isn't exactly waterproof, and you're turning blue." He angled the dashboard heater vents toward her. "See? Warm you up before you catch pneumonia or something."

"F-fine." She pulled the door open, hesitated, and then shot him a stern look. "Just don't try anything funny."

He worked to suppress a grin at her threatening tone. What harm could a woman who looked to be a hundred pounds soaking wet possibly do to him?

She still had yet to climb in, so he raised both hands in the air as a sign of defeat. Legs hesitated a second more, then crawled up into the truck and pulled the door shut behind her. Brent watched as water rained down from her drenched body onto his passenger seat, and thanked the good Lord for the umpteenth time he'd gone with leather upholstery.

"Phone," she demanded and held out a hand.

Nope, still didn't trust him. Ironic, as he was probably the most harmless knight in shining armor around. He handed over the phone, then opened his hand and left it extended toward her. "Brent Masterson, local contractor. Nice to meet you. Again."

Her lashes fluttered. "Oh, uh, Kayla Daniels. Rude stranded traveler. Nice to meet you, too. Again."

As her soft hand pressed into his, the world around them

faded away. The rain, the ice, the worries—everything left his mind but the woman who now sat across from him. She was funny, independent, and, soaking wet or not, hot as hell.

Which made her all the more dangerous.

The instant her hand retracted, the spell was broken. So while she focused on dialing, Brent looked away. It was too easy to stare, to imagine what those curves might look like without the layers of wet clothes plastered to them. What they might feel like.

But he didn't look anymore, didn't feel. Kayla shifted from him as she waited for whoever was on the other end to pick up, and Brent was glad for the additional space between them. Because the further he stayed from her, from anyone, the safer his heart would be.

Kayla dialed Tommy's number and tried to discreetly lean as far away from Brent as possible. Between the soothing, dark interior of his truck and that clean yet spicy aftershave of his, it was a struggle to stay focused. Especially after watching his hips rise off the seat so he could slide a hand into his front right pocket for the phone. That combination had sent her imagination down an entirely different path, one that had nothing to do with cell phones or little brother mechanics.

Get it together, she ordered herself as another ring went by with no answer.

"This is Tommy."

Kayla breathed a sigh of relief and pushed Brent and his hip strength from her mind. "Tommy, it's me. I—"

"Kay? I thought you were on your way home. And what's with the crazy number?"

She snuck a quick glance at Mr. Tall, Dark, and Scowly, whose gaze was trained on the windshield. "Yeah, well, my cell isn't picking up a signal out here, so I had to borrow someone else's. And I was on my way home, but that stupid detour got me all turned around. Then I hit a slick spot and *zoop!* My car slid right off the road."

"And into a fence post I *just* replaced," grumbled Brent.

"Oh my God," Tommy cried. "Are you all right? Is the Impala okay?"

"Yes, I'm fine. The Imp, though, well, she's not budging."

Tommy cursed under his breath. "All right, let me call you a tow. My friend Jimmy owes me a favor, anyway. Just tell me where you are and I'll send him over."

"Where I am?"

Kayla looked out at the bleak, frozen landscape and frowned. She didn't have a clue as to where she was. A quick scan of the countryside for something to use as a point of reference—a billboard, a house, anything—proved worthless. All she could see were freshly tilled fields speckled with clusters of pine trees.

Brent reached over without warning and swiped the phone from her hand. "Tommy? This is Brent Masterson. Yeah, I picked up"—he grimaced—"I mean, *found* your sister wandering down South Whiteville."

He was distracted by the conversation now, allowing Kayla a few seconds to openly gawk at her rescuer's handsome features. His skin was kissed with an early spring tan, or maybe still held color from the countless hours he likely spent outside the year before. He had a straight nose, its size the perfect complement to his high cheekbones and dark brows. Her gaze wandered down his neck, past his broad chest, and followed his long, lean arms. His free hand rested casually on the steering wheel, and the memory of their handshake a moment ago came rushing back. The contact had sent a current rippling through her, a flash of… something.

Intrigue? Desire?

With as long as it'd been since her last venture out into the dating world, it was probably a mixture of both. But his hands felt different from the ones she'd held before. They were large and warm, and callused, too—undoubtedly from years of manual labor. Even so, his grasp had been gentle. Almost too gentle, like he'd been holding back…

"…expecting me. And since I'm late as it is, I'll just have to bring your sister with me," Brent said. "Yeah, send your guy to the Checkerberry Inn. That's where we'll be."

Panic flared in Kayla's chest. Had he just said he was taking her to an *inn*? In the middle of nowhere? She wanted to kick herself for ever climbing into his truck. Now she was trapped.

Or was she? Her gaze flashed to the door handle. Could she get out and bolt before he could catch her?

A hand clamped over her left forearm.

"Don't even think about it, princess."

Kayla yanked her arm free and swallowed hard. "Look, I don't know what kind of girl you think I am, but—"

"I don't know what kind of girl you are," he said, pocketing his phone once more. "Nor do I really care. What I do know is that I've got a lot of work to get done today and not enough hours left to do it. So if you'll fasten your seat belt, we can get going."

"Oh, no." She folded her arms across her chest. "No way. I'm not going to some seedy motel with you."

"A wha—?" He cast a stormy gaze upon her. "The Checkerberry is not and never will be a 'seedy motel'. It's my grandmother's bed-and-breakfast, one of the nicest around. At least, it used to be. Anyway it's warm and dry and where I'm headed. So if you planned on sitting in your car freezing while you wait for a tow truck to arrive, too bad. I'm not turning around."

Kayla stared at him, stunned by his outburst. "Fine."

"Good. Seat belt."

She complied with his order—for her safety, not to please the grump—and resisted the urge to stick out her tongue as she did. The truck started forward, its pace painfully slow. After what seemed like several miles and countless patches of ice later, Brent slowed his vehicle and gingerly turned onto a long, private drive. At its entrance stood a large wooden sign with the words CHECKERBERRY INN painted scarlet and outlined with gold. A picture was carved into the sign below its name, displaying a smooth pond with a deer looking up from its edge. If there was more to the image than that, it was masked beneath a growing layer of ice.

Ice or no, Kayla knew just by looking at the majestic sign that Brent had been telling the truth. Nothing seedy about this place. She shifted her gaze to the frozen green expanse of lawn beside the drive. Hedgerows and rose bushes of varying shapes and sizes dotted the landscape, looking a bit worse for the wear after their winter slumber. Nothing a little spring trimming couldn't remedy. And a good thaw to get rid of all the ice.

Soon a mammoth structure came into view, painted a pale yellow and the size of three colonials placed end to end. The inn was two stories tall, the second level overhanging the first to create a broad, covered porch. Even shrouded by the rain and gloom, it was absolutely beautiful.

"This is your grandmother's?" she breathed.

"It is." Pride tinted his voice.

"Wow."

Brent eased the truck to a stop beside the inn and killed the engine. He cast a quick glance in the backseat, then frowned. "Guess I haven't swapped out my ice scraper for an umbrella yet. Sit tight. I'll run in and grab you one."

He pushed the driver's side door open, jumped out, and made a careful dash up to the inn's covered porch before she had a chance to object. With a sigh, Kayla pushed her own door open and slid to the ground. What good would an umbrella do her? Keep her from getting more soaked?

Determined he not mistake her for the princess type, Kayla carefully made her way up the icy porch steps without him—no small feat in these heels of hers. But soon she was out of the pelting sleet and standing before a large, ornate oak door. A placard displaying the inn's name hung right of the entryway just above the doorbell, giving the entrance a classy look. But much of the rest of the porch had chipped and peeling paint, making the place look a bit more tattered.

Oh, but what a little paint would do for the place. The porch itself hinted of comfort, with a variety of small hooks affixed to its ceiling for hanging porch swings and planters. And the view was nothing short of spectacular. In the distance, rolling green hills were skirted by fields on one side and a thick woods on the other. Flower beds starting to awake from their winter's slumber lay nestled up against every inch of the inn's frontage. And inside them, endless clusters of daffodils.

Daffodils. An all-too-familiar ache pricked at Kayla's heart. She looked away from the ice-covered sunny yellow buds and blinked like mad, intent on keeping her composure. When would she ever get over this ridiculous reaction to some stupid flo—

"I thought I told you to wait in the truck."

She spun around to find Brent with a red and gold golf umbrella in hand. But as he took in the look on her face, the severe angle of his furrowed brows softened, then inverted. Dang it, she hated it when people looked at her like that. Like she was hurting. Because she wasn't, not anymore.

At least, that's what she told herself, each and every day.

Kayla turned from him and swiped a knuckle under each eye. "Did you? I must have missed that part."

His footsteps drew closer, and a fuzzy yellow towel settled on her shoulders. "Here. Why don't you come inside while I try to track down Ruby?"

Again, Mr. Billy Goat Gruff provided a glimpse of his soft underbelly. She was both touched by the gesture and unsettled by it. Kayla wasn't the needy type, and she sure as heck didn't intend to start playing one.

"Thank you. So, who's Ruby? Wait—you call your grandma by her first name?"

A soft chuckle greeted her ears. "Trust me, she wouldn't have it any other way."

Confident her moment of weakness had passed, Kayla turned and caught her hero wearing an honest-to-goodness smile. It crinkled the corners of his eyes and tugged at his hairline, bringing a softness to his features she might otherwise have thought impossible.

He looked younger, approachable. Sexy. For a moment, Kayla forgot how to breathe.

But when he met her gaze, his former stoicism returned. "Come on," he said. "Let's get you inside before you catch your death."

As she watched him walk off without another look back, Kayla wondered if he didn't secretly wish for her to do just that.

Chapter Four

Brent held the inn's front door open and tried his best not to gawk at Kayla's perfect, soaking wet ass as she stepped inside. Tried, but failed. Just like he had tried to avoid her gaze. Those unassuming blues of hers were going to be the end of him—and his self-control.

He needed that tow truck to get here, and get here now.

"Wow…"

She'd stopped, eyes wide as she took in the entryway. Brent felt a surge of pride in his chest. After all the work he'd done renovating this place, a reaction like that never got old.

"Too seedy for you?"

"Are you kidding me?" she said, still drinking in the view. "This place is amazing. It's so open, and bright, and wow…"

Kayla wandered toward the parlor, taking her sweet, floral fragrance with her. If the woman's curiosity was genuine, the room's historical photographs, eclectic furniture, and vast collection of turn-of-the-century board games were sure to keep her occupied for a few minutes. Which, hopefully, would be enough time for him to track down his grandmother. Because while he hoped the tow truck would get here soon, deep down he knew the likelihood of that was slim to none. So the sooner he found Ruby, the sooner he could do the old bait and switch and leave Kayla behind.

Kayla's behind. He dragged a hand over his face. Not what he should be thinking about right now. Later maybe, from the comfort of his own bed. Alone.

"Ruby?" he called, taking the front staircase two steps at a time. Silence greeted him on the second floor. "Ruby?"

Where on earth had she wandered off to on a day like this?

From down below, Brent heard a door open and close. And, judging by the swish that accompanied it, he knew exactly which door it was—one he'd snuck through countless times as a child. Hey, growing boys had to eat. He headed back downstairs, crossed the dining room, and passed through the kitchen's swinging door. Sure enough, his grandmother stood at one of the island countertops, folding linen napkins.

"Ah, there you are."

Ruby looked up from her work and smiled. "Brent, honey, it's so good to see you. Did you get the paint? How was the drive?"

God bless her and her twenty questions, a game she could play with Kayla for the rest of her brief stay. "The paint is in my truck, and the drive was slow." And treacherous, not that he'd admit it. Wouldn't want Ruby to worry about him any more than she already did. "Listen, I could really use your help with something so I can get started on that room remodel upstairs."

"Of course, dear. What do you ne—?"

"Hello? Anybody there?"

Ruby stilled at the sound of the strange voice drifting in from the lobby. "Did your cousin forget to lock the door again?" she said in a harsh whisper. "So help me, I will skin that boy alive the next—"

"Brent?" Kayla called again, her voice closer.

Ruby's brows rose in unison, creating a cascade of wrinkles on her forehead. Brent shot her a pleading look.

"It's not what you think, so don't even start to get your hopes up," he whispered. Too late, of course—the old woman already had that sparkly-eyed look. With a sigh, he nudged the kitchen door back open and called, "Over here."

Ruby came to stand by his side. Upon seeing Kayla, towel wrapped around her shoulders and soaked to the bone, his grandmother donned a grin that would have given the Cheshire Cat a run for his money. Brent threw Ruby a warning look, then wiped it from his face before turning back to their guest.

"Kayla, this is my grandmother, Ruby, the owner of this inn. Ruby, this is Kayla, who was dumb enough to be out on the road today and slammed her car into that new fence post of Bob's I just replaced."

Kayla's cheeks turned pink. Brent felt a small stab of guilt but pushed it aside. It was better if she didn't become too attached to him.

"Now is that any way to talk to a young lady? Honestly, Brent, where are your manners?" Ruby swatted him in the arm, then turned her attention back to Kayla. "Hello dear, so very nice to meet you. I'm terribly sorry to hear about your accident. Are you hurt?"

"No, I'm fine, thank you. Things could have ended a whole lot worse—it's awfully slick out there."

"Which is why you shouldn't have been driving in the first place," Brent said under his breath.

"Maybe I didn't have a choice," Kayla muttered back.

Ruby eyed them both. "I take it your car is stuck?"

"Yes," Kayla said. "But my brother called for a tow truck. It should be on its way."

"Oh, I wouldn't count on them getting your car back on the road any time soon, dear. With weather like this, it may be a while." Ruby studied Kayla for a moment, the look in her eyes soft. Motherly. "Do you have a bag with you? Perhaps some dry clothes to change into?"

"No, actually I don't," said Kayla. "My trip to Mount Pleasant was sort of a spur-of-the-moment thing."

"Well, we can't have you standing around all soaking wet, now can we?" Ruby said.

"But I—"

"No buts, young lady." Ruby took Kayla by the elbow. "Come along upstairs with me, and we'll see if we can't find something to make do while we get your clothes dried. And I think a hot shower will do you a world of good."

"I really wouldn't want to put you out."

Kayla shot Brent a pleading look, but he just shrugged and offered her a look of mock innocence. He knew better than to argue with Ruby, especially when she was in mothering mode. If there was one thing Ruby loved more than the inn, it was mothering people. And who was Brent to deny her such a thing, especially when it meant taking one all-too-alluring little vixen off his hands?

Kayla stood beneath a massaging stream of hot water in one of the Checkerberry's amazing upstairs suites and felt like she'd died and gone to heaven. The cloud of steam swirling around her only added to the illusion. She hadn't realized how cold she'd been until she first stepped under the hot water's spray and nearly cried out from the pain. It was like a hundred bees, stinging her all at once. Eventually, though, she'd managed to ease her way in and thawed out.

Now warm and squeaky-clean—thanks to the aromatic array of soaps, shampoos, and conditioners Ruby kept stocked in here—Kayla was still reluctant to turn off the faucet. Once her shower ended, she'd have to face the real world again. An unfair world, where innocent employees got framed, cars ate fence posts, and heroes were handsome grouches.

Not exactly anything she wanted to hurry back to.

But after a few more minutes, her growing guilt for hogging the inn's hot water got the best of her. She dried off, then dug into her purse for an emergency hairbrush and what little makeup she had with her. Not that it really mattered. No one around here cared what she looked like, or knew any better. So far they'd only ever seen her at her worst; anything had to be an improvement.

Ah, but that wasn't entirely true. Brent had seen her at the diner. The memory of their encounter instantly came to mind. His solid chest. Strong arms. Stormy gray eyes. Grouch or not, there was something about his intense gaze that woke up long-dormant parts of her. Girly parts. Parts that had absolutely no business waking up in the middle of this utter mess called Friday.

Still, a little mascara never hurt anyone…

Fresh-faced and with a towel wrapped securely around her, Kayla cracked open the bathroom door and peered out. Just as Ruby had promised, her soaking wet clothes were gone. The only article of clothing in sight was a fluffy white terrycloth robe, neatly folded and perched on the edge of the suite's bed, with a handwritten note on top.

> *Make yourself at home. This robe should keep you*
> *warm while your clothes are in the wash. —Ruby*

"Wash?" Kayla whispered, her newfound calm starting to slip away. Washing would take too long. What if the tow truck arrived before her clothes were done? She couldn't exactly jump into the tow truck to show the driver to her car dressed like this.

Kayla closed her eyes and dragged a long, slow breath in and then back out. *Think positive.* Maybe the wash would be done before Jimmy and his tow truck came to her rescue. That's what Ruby had suggested, anyway. Until then, she'd just hang out up here. Maybe take a little nap.

Her gaze shifted to the bed. It did look awfully inviting, with its patchwork quilt in varying shades of coastal blues and the cluster of matching pillows above. She sat down on its edge to test it out. Not too hard, not too soft. Yep, the perfect mattress for napping on a rainy day.

A knock sounded. "All better, dear?"

Kayla sprang from the bed and hurried to the door. She pulled it open a crack, peeked out to make sure Ruby was the only one in sight, and then opened it another foot or so.

"Yes, thank you. You were right—I feel a million times better."

"Wonderful. Then why don't you come downstairs and get a little something to eat now?"

Kayla glanced up and down the hall. Could she really walk out there, wearing only a robe? That's when she looked down, and realized she had yet to put on the robe. With a grimace, she shifted her towel-covered torso so that more of it was hidden by the door.

"Um, thanks, Ruby. But I'm not really that hungry."

"Nonsense. After all the shivering you did, we need to get some food in your belly. Wouldn't want you fainting from low blood sugar, now would we?"

"Well, no, but—"

"Good. I've got some snacks set out in the dining room for you. Come down when you're ready."

Ruby shuffled away without another look back, and Kayla knew the battle had been lost. Why hadn't she just asked Ruby to bring her the food? Because that would have been rude, she thought, and would have made her look like some helpless, needy little girl. Of which she was neither.

She shut the door and crossed the room to trade her towel for the robe. Robe? A tent was more like it. The darned thing was so big she had to roll up both sleeves just to find her hands. Kayla wrapped it around her as best she could and checked her reflection in the mirror. She looked…hideous.

Doesn't matter, she reminded herself. She wasn't there to impress anyone. Especially not the hunky handyman.

Now if only she could make herself believe that.

F inally.

Brent loved his grandmother, but when it came to getting work done, she was the politest disruption alive. Not that he could really blame her. Ruby was a social being—she thrived on interacting with others. Which made the off-season a particularly difficult time for her. And him, when his cousin wasn't here to keep her company.

Where the hell is Miles, anyway? he wondered as he hurried inside with the last of the paint supplies. Damn idiot better not have slid into a ditch, too. Because if that was the case, he could just walk his ass back to the inn—Brent was already an hour behind in his work. And just because the rain had delayed their painting of the barn didn't mean there weren't plenty of rooms inside that still needed a few coats of paint.

Which was probably why his cousin was nowhere to be found.

Brent headed for the stairs but stopped at their base to allow his descending grandmother to pass.

"Hungry, dear?"

"No. Thank you."

"*Tsk, tsk, tsk*. Going to waste away." She patted his belly as she passed.

Not likely, he thought with a grin, remembering the veritable feast o' grease he'd consumed earlier at EAT.

"If you change your mind," she said without stopping, "there are snacks in the dining room. Kayla will be down shortly."

Christ. Leave it to Ruby to take any opportunity she got to try and play matchmaker. Because that's exactly what this offering of a snack was. He eyed the staircase.

The coast was still clear.

With a new sense of urgency, he made his way up the stairs with both arms full of paint supplies. When he reached the oversized landing, which also served as a sitting area, he paused. Looked and listened.

Still no sign of her. Relief washed over Brent. A few more steps and he'd be past her room. Once he made it to the Blueberry Suite, he could close the door and lose himself in his work. If he were lucky, the tow truck would be here and long gone with her before he finished.

And that would be the only way he'd get lucky today. Judging by her skittish behavior in the car, no way would Kayla let him get close to her again. Which was for the best, he told himself. Repeatedly.

Two steps past the landing, the bag of rollers and brushes he'd wedged under one arm decided to go Kamikaze. With a curse, he stooped to set down his paint cans, then scrambled to retrieve the AWOL items.

One roller cover. Two. Damn, where was the third? He scanned the landing, then crouched down to check under the nearest furniture.

"Looking for something?"

Brent's head jerked up at the sound and slammed into the edge of an end table. He bit back a stream of profanity and waited for the stars to disappear from his vision. As they did, he froze.

He'd been right to want to hurry past Kayla's room. She

stood before him now, barefoot and nearly irresistible in a white, oversized bathrobe. Adorable and tantalizing all at the same time. How was that even possible?

"Uh, yeah." He cleared his throat and shifted his gaze back to the floor. "Rogue paint roller. I'm sure it's around here somewhere."

"You mean this?"

He shouldn't have looked. Should have kept his eyes fixed on the floor before him. But, hey, he was male and had a pulse. So his traitorous gaze flashed to her as she bent down to grasp the roller cover at her feet. The top of her robe gaped at the movement, providing him another accidental peek at her cleavage, still rosy pink from her shower.

She gripped the base of the tube, stood, and brought it to him. "Here you go."

"Thanks."

He collected the rest of his supplies and headed for the hall without another word. The less interaction he had with Kayla, the less tempted he'd be to get to know her. He'd given up long ago on dating or allowing himself to care about anyone outside their family, and now was definitely not the time to go changing that. The tow truck would be here soon enough, and then she'd be gone.

Because that's what the women in his life always did.

They left.

Chapter Five

Kayla hit the bottom step of the front staircase and kept right on going. She didn't look back, didn't pause to catch one more glimpse of Brent. What was it about him that seemed to turn her on and tick her off at the same time?

Okay, so maybe it'd been a while since she'd been with anyone besides Big Red. As in months and months. But vibrators never told you to shush when the game came back on, or complained when you threw away their favorite two-year-old fantasy football magazine.

Men.

Kayla padded into the dining room in her bare feet and looked around for Ruby. The white-haired hostess was nowhere to be seen, but a small feast had been set out on a table along one wall of the room. Deli meats and cheeses, artisan bread, diced fruit, and small pastries had her stomach suddenly growling.

Ruby stepped out from the kitchen and spied her.

"Feeling better, dear?"

"Yes, thank you. I feel like a whole new me." She tugged at the top of her robe. "Will feel even better once I'm back in my own clothes, though."

"Poo!" Ruby said, walking around Kayla. She set down a notebook and pen, then picked up a plate from the stack beside the mini feast and handed it to her. "No one here is going to judge you by what you're wearing. So you just get some food in that skinny little body of yours and relax a while. Happy and comfortable, that's how my guests should feel."

Kayla took the plate and smiled. "Well, okay then."

She made herself a ham and cheese sandwich, scooped up a small bowl of fruit, then headed to a table near the windows with both. Ruby poured her a glass of ice water and followed along.

"Would you like me to brew a fresh pot of coffee?" She set the water down by Kayla's place setting. "I'd be happy to."

"No," Kayla said. "Water's fine, thank you."

"All right. But if you change your mind, let me know."

With that, Ruby collected her things and disappeared behind the kitchen door once more. That left the dining room silent, save for the *plink, plink, plink* of freezing rain still falling. Kayla allowed herself to get lost in the wintery scene outside as she ate. Being there, in the middle of nowhere at an inn blanketed by ice, gave her an odd sense of peace. It was as though she were untouchable to all her troubles back home, even if just for a little while.

And, boy, did she have troubles back home. The memory of her horrid morning returned, bringing with it dark thoughts about Wayne Advertising. How could Joe have stooped so low? And why hadn't her boss given her a chance to explain? But the bigger question she faced now was whether or not her dream career was salvageable.

"All finished?"

Kayla turned from the window and offered her hostess a smile. "Yes. Thank you, Ruby. That was just perfect."

"Wonderful! Did my grandson ever make it down to join you?" Ruby craned her neck toward the lobby.

"No. Was...he supposed to?"

"That boy never listens," Ruby said, shaking her head. "He'd starve himself to death if I didn't keep reminding him to eat. Work, work, work, that's all he ever does."

Kayla grimaced. She could relate.

"And he works here, for you?"

Ruby settled into a chair at Kayla's table. "Yes. Well, before this spring it was just when I needed him for special projects. He had his own business then. But our groundskeeper resigned a few weeks ago, and Brent insisted he could do the job himself. Such a good boy."

"That was very sweet of him. He must really love his grandmother." She gave Ruby a wink.

"Nothing to be ashamed of," Ruby said and winked back.

Kayla had been fond of Ruby since the moment they met. The spunky senior had been nothing but kind to her, treating her from the beginning like one of the fold. It made Kayla miss her own long-deceased grandparents even more. And her mother, who would have adored Ruby, too.

Careful to keep her emotions in check, Kayla glanced around the large dining area. What might it look like, full of summertime guests? Would there be families with babies and toddlers, middle-aged couples on weekend getaways, or retirees traveling town to town as they saw fit? She cast a curious look at Ruby.

"Can I ask you something?"

"Absolutely."

"What's it like, running a place like this?"

"Like every day is an adventure," Ruby answered, her voice reverent and a twinkle in her eyes. "New guests and old, each here for different reasons, different durations. And all with their own stories, their own personalities. People come from all over the country to stay here, you know. Why, we've even had a few families from Europe seek us out."

"Europe?"

Ruby nodded. "Just England and Germany so far. They had friends from the States who'd stayed here and recommended the Checkerberry. You can imagine how tickled I was when I heard that."

She paused, her gaze on the entryway. After a moment, she sighed and looked back to Kayla. The sparkle in her eyes had faded.

"Unfortunately, people just haven't been coming here as often the past few years. Before, we'd have every suite booked and a growing waiting list before opening day. Now, we're lucky to fill half our rooms on non-holiday weeks."

"I'm sorry to hear that."

"Oh, don't worry about us, dear," Ruby said, reaching out to pat her hand. "Every inn has its highs and lows, and we've survived both. Unfortunately, not everyone on my staff is as confident as me."

"Why aren't people coming back, do you think?"

Ruby shrugged. "My guess is it's a combination of things. Bad economy. Price of gas keeps rising. Lowered expectations. People see all these cookie-cutter hotels right off the highway where they can sleep cheap, so they go there and settle for rooms with minimal amenities and window views of the hotel next door.

"Inundated by commercials and billboards, so many travelers have forgotten it doesn't have to be that way. Out here, they have gorgeous views from every window. Cozy seats by the fire inside, or on a lounge chair outside. No crowds, no noisy traffic. Just peace and quiet."

"Well, I'd pick your inn over some stuffy hotel any day, if I were on vacation," Kayla said.

She looked around the dining room once more, with its high ceilings and ornate parquet floor, and felt an unexpected compulsion to help Ruby fill it to bursting once more. But what could she possibly do? Kayla knew nothing about running a hotel. Heck, she didn't even have her computer on her—it was still in the backseat of her car.

Her car.

Kayla's gaze shifted to a large clock hanging on a wall across the way. What she really should be doing was finding a way to turn the tables on that SOB Joe and get her suspension lifted, not out trying to rescue little old ladies and their aging bed-and-breakfasts. If she wanted to pay her rent this month, anyway. Now where was that tow truck?

"Well, thank you, dear. Perhaps you can come back for a visit sometime soon." Ruby rose to her feet. "Why don't I go and check on those clothes of yours, hmm? Your ride should be along any time now."

"Thank you." Kayla stood as well, and picked up her plate, fork, and glass. "Where would you like these?"

"You can just leave them there, dear."

"Please," she said, stepping forward. "I've put you out

enough as it is. Let me help clean up."

The ghost of a grin tugged at the soft wrinkles around her hostess's lips. "If you insist. Just set the dishes in the kitchen next to the sink. The trays with food still on them can go on the island in the middle of the kitchen. I'll wrap those up. They'll be gone soon enough, once my grandsons sniff them out."

"Sniff what out?"

Both women turned their heads toward the new voice. A warmer, jovial tenor than that of the grouchy handyman. The newcomer standing in their midst looked nothing like Brent, either. This man was tall and lean with stylish light brown hair and chocolate eyes. His face was smooth and slightly tanned, his smile wide and welcoming.

"Miles, dear, you're just in time to help," said Ruby.

"Oh?" His gaze met Kayla's, then dipped briefly to her robe and back. "Well, you know how I love to help. Any way I can."

Kayla swallowed hard. Heaven help her. If this was yet another grandson, Ruby needed to change the name of this place from Checkerberry Inn to Temptation Inn.

B rent finished rolling primer in the Blueberry Suite, then stepped back and dragged a hand across his damp forehead. He'd worked up one hell of a sweat trying to make up for lost time. And to keep Kayla off his mind.

But now that he'd stopped to take a break, all that white on the walls had him thinking about a certain terrycloth robe and the shower-fresh skin beneath it. *Nope, don't go there*, he told himself. Not gonna happen. With a frustrated sigh, he set down his roller and headed into the suite's bathroom to wash up.

Only the room had been stripped bare. No soap, no towels, no nothing.

Of course not, you idiot—you cleared all of that out yesterday. Prepping to paint, remember?

Brent muttered a few choice words about his predicament, then turned and made his way downstairs. He'd worked up an appetite. Might as well take a short break and grab a bite to eat.

Hungry. Yep, that was his story, and he was sticking to it. Had nothing to do with checking to see if their robe-wearing stranded motorist had left yet or not. Or that he hoped she had, nearly as much as he hoped she hadn't.

As Brent headed downstairs and through the lobby, muffled laughter greeted his ears, the sound high and musical. He couldn't help but smile, envisioning Ruby in her element, entertaining and mothering. But his smile faded as the sound of a third voice chimed in.

A voice that belonged to his playboy cousin.

Brent shoved the kitchen's swinging door open. Three faces turned toward him in surprise, their expressions frozen in place.

"What's this? A party, and no one invited me?" His gaze settled on Kayla, who quickly looked away.

"Oh, so now you're the partying type?" Miles said from beside her. "Shall I send out a press release?"

"Miles," Ruby chided, then turned toward Brent. "How's your painting going, dear?"

"Fine," he grumbled. "Would have gotten more done if

worthless over there had helped like he'd promised."

"Now, cousin. Is that how we talk to our guests?" Miles draped an arm around Kayla's robed shoulders.

Brent found neither the humor nor the gesture amusing, and anger began to boil up inside him. Which was ridiculous, of course. She didn't belong to him. Didn't belong to any of them. In fact, they'd all be better off when she was long gone.

"I wasn't talking to her, I was talking to you. And she's not our guest. More like a visitor. A *temporary* visitor."

The words came out sounding harsher than he'd intended, and Kayla's cheeks flushed a deep shade of red. For once he wished he could be more like Miles: easygoing and a natural with the opposite sex. Then maybe he wouldn't keep coming off sounding like a total dick.

"Well, as long as she's here," Ruby said, her voice taking on the calm, detached tone which always preluded a later lecture, "you will treat her with courtesy and respect."

"Yes, ma'am," Brent muttered, then made his way across the room to the utility sink.

The old sink and the washer and dryer next to it always reminded him of his grandfather. John Masterson had been a good man and a hard worker. He'd always put his family's needs before his own and rarely let his temper get the best of him. All qualities that Brent worked hard to emulate. Some days, that was an easier task than others.

Still, he couldn't help but think if his grandfather were here now, he would have told Miles to stop flirting and get to work. The thought brought Brent a small amount of comfort. Damn, he missed the old codger. Missed his folks even more. Would probably miss Miles, too, if he ever stopped threatening to leave town and actually did it.

He shot a quick glance back in his cousin's direction. Miles's arm was still draped over Kayla's shoulders.

Nah, probably not.

He tried to tune out the others as he scrubbed away the paint splatter from his forearms. Yet another reason he hated painting. Too bad old Jackson had quit on them. Painting never seemed to bother him…

The inn's phone sprang to life, and the banter behind him quieted.

"Checkerberry Inn, how may we help you?" Ruby asked. "Ah, yes, she's here. One moment, please."

Brent held his breath. It was the tow truck driver. Had to be. Soon Kayla would be gone, and life at the Checkerberry could get back to normal.

"This is Kayla. Yes, that was my brother. Really? Oh. Wow. Yes, I understand."

Disappointment rang clear in her words. Damn towing company was probably giving her the runaround. The freezing rain had changed back to a regular drizzle about half an hour ago, which would clear the roads of ice soon enough. She needed to get going before it got dark and the cooler overnight temperatures froze everything all over again. And before any of the fools here offered to let her stay.

Because she definitely couldn't stay. Oh, no. It was all he could do to resist her now—no way he'd be able to stick around if she stayed overnight. Nor did he trust his cousin to stay, either. Not with the way Miles was eyeing Kayla as though he were a drunk and she was a bottle of perfectly aged whiskey.

"Well, can you at least give me some kind of idea when it might be?" Kayla asked into the phone. "Yes, I-I understand.

I'll wait to hear from you, then. Good-bye."

"Tow truck running behind?" asked Miles.

Brent attacked the paint on his arms with new vigor. The sincerity in Miles's voice was a trademark move. Nine times out of ten, it worked. Usually what happened between his cousin and the general female population was of little interest to Brent. So why was he so bothered by it now? What made Kayla any different than the rest?

To that question, he had no answer. Only that she was different, because he'd noticed her. And it'd been a long time since anyone worth noticing had walked into his life. God, he had to get her out of here before he did something stupid. Like take her to bed and ravish her. All. Night. Long. He turned the water to cold, splashed some onto his face hoping the shock would clear his head, then reached for a towel.

"Yeah. Really late. As in, they're swamped and can't get here until tomorrow."

Brent spun around. "Tomorrow?"

Kayla met his gaze. She looked so disappointed, so vulnerable. The urge to cross the room and comfort her washed over him.

Comfort her?

Shit.

He dabbed at his face with the towel. Tried to appear cool, calm. "Well then, we should get you into town. Find you a place at the Red Roof Inn or the Courtyard, before they get swamped with a bunch of other stranded drivers."

Kayla flinched. It was a subtle movement, so subtle the others may not have even noticed. But he had. He was far too in tune with her movements, her nonverbal cues. He hated to treat her this way, but she'd thank him for pushing her away later.

"But, I really can't—"

"And what is the Checkerberry?" Ruby planted both hands on her hips. "Chopped liver?"

"Of course not. It's just that we're not technically open"—*and she's sure to be the end of me*—"and I assumed you wouldn't want to—"

"Well, you assumed wrong." Ruby shot him a dark look, then turned and offered Kayla a gentle smile. "I'm very sorry to hear about the delay, dear. I know you were eager to return home yet tonight. But you are more than welcome to stay here until the tow truck arrives."

Kayla hesitated, and Brent felt a glimmer of hope that she might actually turn down Ruby's offer. But then his grandmother played dirty. She took Kayla's hand in hers and gave their visitor the "poor old innkeeper" eyes.

No one could resist those, not even him.

"Please won't you stay? It's so lonely in the off-season, and I'd love to have some female company. And you really can't beat free, now can you?"

"Are you sure I wouldn't be imposing on you?"

Why had Kayla looked directly at him when she said that?

"Heavens, no. Why, if you stay, I'll see that you're treated like royalty. When was the last time you felt like that?"

"Royalty?" Kayla laughed. "Hmm, let me think. That'd be, oh, never."

"Then it's settled," Ruby said. She rambled on about possible dinner selections and things to do during Kayla's stay. Soon everyone was smiling and carrying on.

Everyone, that is, except Brent.

Chapter Six

Treated like royalty…

Kayla smiled at the thought as she stretched beneath the covers of her suite's incredibly comfortable queen-sized bed. The pre-dinner nap had done her a world of good, and she woke feeling both rested and relaxed. *Like a queen*, she thought with a giggle as she eyed the mountain of motley pillows she'd pushed aside to find the top edge of the comforter. Ruby was right—travelers had lowered their standards.

One afternoon at the inn and hotel life for Kayla had been ruined. Not that she traveled all that much, anyway. No time to, when she spent most of her waking hours working, either at the office or her father's place. Or thinking about work. Or thinking about thinking about work.

You need to get a life, whispered a voice in the back of her mind. Lying there, snug as a bug beneath luxurious Egyptian cotton sheets, Kayla stared up at the ceiling and pondered that thought. A life? Outside of work? One that actually involved other human beings, not just her laptop and cell phone?

Ah, but that might lead to her getting emotionally attached to someone. With a sigh, she pushed the covers back and crawled out of bed. Kayla didn't want to get attached, didn't want to rely on anyone ever again. Though that'd be a tough decision to stick to if she lived around here, what with Ruby's two grandsons being ridiculously gorgeous and all. Was it something in the water or just a stellar gene pool?

No matter, she'd be gone soon enough.

Kayla crossed the room to her freshly washed and dried clothes and dressed in all but her long-discarded panty hose. Nope, those puppies were unsalvageable. *Good riddance*, she thought with a grin as she headed into the bathroom to finish getting ready before going down to dinner.

No flatiron meant nothing to straighten her unruly natural waves, so she settled for pulling her hair up in a twist and locking it into place with the emergency clip she kept in her purse. A few tendrils of hair refused to be confined, but without extra pins or hairspray, she let them be. She touched up her makeup, then checked her reflection in the mirror one last time before heading downstairs.

It wasn't her best look, but it'd have to do. After the wet rat look she'd sported earlier, anything at this point had to be an improvement, right? Not that she cared what the others thought of her. Much.

"Did you enjoy your nap, dear?" Ruby asked as she walked Kayla to a round-topped table in the dining room's center. She wore her hair up as well, and had changed into a long chambray skirt and thick cable-knit sweater.

"Oh, yes. That bed is amazing. I'd come back to visit just for that," Kayla said with a laugh. She caught sight of Miles then, entering the dining room as well. Apparently dinnertime at the Checkerberry was taken seriously, as he had also changed his attire. Gone were his designer jeans and burgundy Henley, replaced with navy slacks and a crisp buttondown shirt. His all-too-appealing smile, however, remained.

With a cough, she ceased her giggling and pulled a chair out from the table.

"Please," he said, stepping around her and grasping the chair's back. "Allow me."

"See?" Ruby said with a wink. "Like royalty."

"Uh-huh. And do all your guests get treated with such courtesy?"

"Of course," Ruby said, then started for the kitchen once more, mumbling about dinner rolls as she walked.

"Nah, only the pretty ones," Miles whispered as he pushed her chair forward.

Kayla felt her cheeks warm. Miles was charming, she'd give him that. And easy on the eyes. Very easy. But her mind kept wandering back to his cousin, her roadside hero. Which was silly. Brent clearly had no interest in her. *Miles, on the other hand…*

She grinned. Maybe a little harmless flirting with him would help push Brent from her mind.

"Wine?" Miles asked, stepping back.

"Sure. Something sweet?"

"I would have guessed as much," he said with a grin. "Let me see what Ruby's got over here." He crossed the room and bent to assess some hidden collection stored behind a small, six-seater bar top. "Hmm, looks like she's got Chardonnay, white Zinfandel, and—"

"White Zinfandel is fine, thanks."

As he worked the corkscrew, Ruby burst through the kitchen doors with a basket of steaming rolls.

"Oh, thank you, Miles. I meant to get that out earlier." She set the basket on their table and then looked around with a scowl. "Where is your cousin?"

"I don't think he was planning on joining us." Miles crossed the room with the open bottle of wine. "Something about not having a change of clothes."

Kayla reached for the glass of ice water nearest her place setting. No Brent meant no scowling. Still, she felt an unexpected pang of disappointment.

"He is not going to talk his way out of this," Ruby growled. "I don't care if he has to sit here naked, that boy is going to eat."

Naked? Kayla's drink of water went down the wrong pipe. Ruby patted her back until the coughing fit subsided, then marched from the room.

"You gonna live?" Miles handed her a glass of wine and reached to refill her water.

"Maybe." She downed the drink as if it were water, trying to drown out the image Ruby's comment had summoned—Brent strutting into the room wearing nothing but his birthday suit. When she spoke again, her voice was rough from the wine…and that image. "Thanks. I, um, love white Zin."

"I can see that," Miles said with a chuckle.

Wine glass in hand he took the seat across from her. Kayla smiled at him to prove she would survive and reached for a roll. When it came to drinking, she'd always been a lightweight. The last thing she wanted to do was get drunk before the main course arrived—Lord only knew what might come out of her mouth if that happened.

"Where did you say you were from again?" he asked.

"Fort Wayne. It's a few hours south of here."

"And you're here on business?"

More like avoiding it… "No, I came to visit my—"

Ruby shuffled back into the room, muttering something under her breath. When she saw Miles and Kayla looking at her, she offered them a quick smile. "Sorry for the delay, dinner will be ready momentarily. I just hate to start without everyone."

"You're wasting your time, Grandma," Miles said casually. "Brent's stubborn as—"

"A mule?" Brent finished, appearing in the doorway.

Kayla froze, a small piece of roll raised halfway to her mouth. The standoffish handyman still wore his familiar scowl, and the same paint-splattered jeans, faded in all the right places from wear, but he'd pulled an expensive-looking, black V-neck sweater on over his T-shirt. A sweater he filled out quite nicely.

Too nicely, in fact.

Kayla traded her dinner roll for the wine glass and took a good, long drink.

B rent leveled a look at his cousin. "Better to be as stubborn as a mule than to actually *be* one, Miles. You, of all people, should know that."

He made his way to their table and took the empty seat

to Kayla's left, careful not to meet her gaze. Those blue eyes of hers had a way of breaking through his defenses. Unfortunately, Ruby had threatened to drag him to dinner by his ear if he didn't join them. And she'd dragged him around by his ear enough times in his youth for him to know how damned much that hurt.

Though now that he was here, he wondered which would have truly been more painful: the ear pulling, or sitting beside a beautiful siren all through dinner. She was back in her corporate clothes, that purple blouse unbuttoned just far enough to be respectable but still managing to tease and the hip-hugging skirt that begged to be pushed up and out of the way. And now, as if to torture him further, she'd gone and pulled her hair up, leaving her perfect neck exposed, save for a few delicate stray curls. A neck waiting to be explored, along with every inch of the rest of her.

"Ah, I see Ruby found you something to wear after all," Miles said, with a smirk. "So nice of you to join us, by the way."

"I didn't have much of a choice."

"Well, it's a good thing you had that sweater handy. Ruby threatened to make you sit here in the nude."

The roll in Kayla's hand dropped to her plate. Her cheeks flushed scarlet. "Speaking of Ruby, maybe I should go and see if she needs help."

"No!" he and Miles answered in unison. They exchanged a quick look, silently posturing to see who should be the one to leave Kayla to go and help their grandmother. When Brent didn't budge, Miles's brows rose. As a grin stretched across his cousin's face, Brent knew he'd be hearing about this later.

Miles pushed his chair back from the table and stood. "I'll go. She'd kill us if we let you lift a finger."

He headed for the kitchen with a wink, and an awkward silence ensued. Brent could have kicked himself. Why hadn't he volunteered? Miles was the Masterson who could keep conversations rolling, not him.

Brent reached for his water glass and took a drink, then cast another look at the kitchen door. Any minute now the rest of his family would reappear with dinner in hand. Any. Minute. Now.

"Roll?"

He looked up in surprise and was instantly trapped in the snare of those unassuming blue eyes.

"Sure," he said, forcing his gaze from hers to the basket of rolls in her extended hand. "Thank you."

Kayla took another roll herself and set the basket on the table. The silence resumed, though twice she looked as though she wanted to say something, then chose not to. Brent knew he should speak up, but couldn't think of anything to say. When it came to social graces, Miles definitely had him beat hands down.

And where the hell had he and Ruby gone, anyway?

"So, how did your painting go?"

"Hmm?" His gaze cut away from the door again and back to hers. "Oh, good. Got a bedroom done and a bath-room primed. May even be able to get a first coat on it yet tonight."

"Nice. Did you have a lot of cutting in to do, or mostly rolling?"

Spoken like a painting veteran, Brent thought with a grin. Maybe she wasn't a helpless princess after all.

"Lots of cutting in. Which in and of itself isn't so bad. It's trying to wedge a stepladder in around a tub and toilet that I hate."

"I hear you," she said. "I painted my brother's bathroom last fall and nearly broke my neck trying to reach over the shower walls."

"Why were you painting your brother's bathroom?"

Kayla scowled. "I lost a bet. Said Central Michigan couldn't beat U of M. Darn Wolverines."

Brent chuckled. "You're a Michigan fan?"

"Oh, no, I'm an IU grad. Well, IPFW, actually, but my degree says Indiana University. I just figured a school from the Big Ten Conference could handle Central Michigan. Guess I was wrong."

"Yeah, U of M has had a few tough years." Brent began to find those blue eyes a little less intimidating. He leaned forward, resting his elbows on the edge of the table. "So, your brother lives up here and you live where again?"

"Fort Wayne, Indiana."

"I've been there before. Helped move a buddy from college down there a few years back. And your folks? Where do they live?"

Kayla's smile faltered as her gaze shifted to the tabletop. "My dad lives not too far from me."

Shit. He'd gone and upset her. This was why he let Miles do the talking.

As if on cue, his cousin reentered the room followed closely by Ruby, each carrying steaming casserole dishes. Between the mouth-watering aroma of Ruby's chicken marmalade and the light banter between her and Miles, the mood in the room quickly returned to its lighthearted state.

Brent remained quiet for most of the meal, choosing instead to sit back and observe her interactions with his family. He'd been wrong about her at the diner. Kayla was a vibrant, sweet, funny young woman. But something in her past was haunting her—that flash of hurt in her eyes at the mention of her parents hadn't been lost on him.

Hurt was an emotional state he knew all too well, and one Brent made a silent promise not to inflict on her again.

Once the others rejoined their table, Kayla allowed herself to relax. To let go.

To forget.

Her social life back home was limited, her friendships guarded and minimal. It was easier that way. Safer. But here, among strangers, she felt liberated to let her guard down. To be silly and engaged, absorbed and entertained. To just…be. Those around her had done the same, sharing stories and listening to her own. The mood stayed light, and though Brent remained reserved throughout their meal, even he was smiling by the time dessert rolled around. A smile, Kayla couldn't help but notice, made him all the more handsome.

But after the chocolate torte and decaf coffee had been consumed, she was saddened to see fatigue overshadow her companions' faces. Kayla didn't want the evening to end. Didn't want to go back to her room, to reality. She hadn't felt this free in years.

"Please let me help with the dishes, Ruby."

Her hostess swatted Kayla's hand from her empty plate. "Absolutely not. My guests don't lift a finger. Like royalty, remember?"

With a grin, Brent met Kayla's gaze. And as they'd done so time and time again throughout dinner, his stormy gray eyes took her breath away. Clearly he was oblivious to the power those eyes could wield, unlike his equally handsome cousin. Miles was funny and charming and knew it, too. Some women found that kind of self-confidence appealing, but guys like that weren't really Kayla's type.

Though it'd been so long since she'd put herself out there she wasn't sure if she even knew what her type was anymore. All she'd cozied up to in recent months was her laptop, the universal remote, and Big Red—which she was doing her best not to think about right now, trapped by Brent's stare.

Breathe, she reminded herself. *And blink. Blinking would be good.*

Brent's gaze shifted from hers. "I'll help you, Ruby."

The innkeeper batted his hand away as well. "No, Miles can help me with all of this."

Miles frowned. "But—"

"No buts, young man. You skirted your responsibilities earlier, so you'll just have to make up for it by helping me in the kitchen."

Kayla giggled as Miles's shoulders slumped. She yawned, but remained seated. Maybe she could just sit a while longer. Stare at the artwork on the walls or something while her libido cooled back down.

"Ah, a yawn—now that's the sign of a happy stomach. Brent, why don't you see that Kayla makes it back to her room okay? Oh, and I don't want anyone driving home in this mess. You can stay in the Strawberry Suite upstairs; it's got fresh linens and towels, and Miles, you can take the

Bourbon Room down here.

Wait, had Ruby just told Brent to stay in a room upstairs? Near hers? Kayla shot a look of alarm at Brent. He opened his mouth, hesitated, then snapped it shut, his lips drawing into a thin line. Ruby had already turned away and was walking back to the kitchen with a casserole dish in her hands. Miles stood and snagged a few plates, then followed after her, grumbling under his breath about the unfairness of it all along the way.

She watched them go, panic rising in her chest. Upstairs. With Brent.

He cleared his throat, and she looked over to find his trademark scowl had returned. It seemed she wasn't the only one unsettled by Ruby's room assignments. He stood and motioned toward the lobby, looking like a schoolboy performing a chore.

"After you."

"I'm fully capable of finding my way back, thank you very much."

She lifted her chin in defiance and stood. A zing of pain shot through her left foot, the consequence of sitting with her legs crossed for far too long. Refusing to admit her weakened state, she pushed her own chair back and moved to step around it. Unfortunately, her foot might as well have been made of Jell-O. Brent caught her as she lurched forward.

"That may be up for debate," he said, amusement playing in his low voice.

His grasp was strong yet gentle, careful yet capable. Just like it'd been at the diner. Kayla swallowed hard and pulled back from him. The pins and needles feeling in her foot was already beginning to subside.

"Really, I'm fine."

"Regardless, I've been tasked with seeing you to your room."

Tasked. He sure knew how to make a lady feel special. Kayla tested to make sure her ankle would cooperate, then started for the lobby.

"Your grandmother really does rule the roost, doesn't she?"

"It is her inn."

Touché.

They mounted the stairs, her before him. He stayed close, as though unconvinced she could make it on her own, and his cologne tickled at her senses. Senses that became more alert with each step she took. Brent remained silent, an unspoken yet palpable tension growing between them.

What *was* it about this man that left her so unsettled?

Kayla reached the landing and continued on to the hall. A few more steps and she'd be away from the tension, away from the scowls. But when they reached her suite she paused, torn. Behind the closed door was a night full of what so many before had held: loneliness. And for the first time in forever, she longed for something more. A playful grin tugged at her lips.

"So, you've been assigned the room beside mine, huh?"

Oh, she was playing with fire, and she knew it. But desperate times called for desperate measures. She couldn't spend all evening in there, alone with her thoughts and worries. Brent stared down at her and said nothing, his right brow raised but eyes unreadable.

"Oh, that's right. It's her inn." She was taunting him now,

and enjoying the heck out of herself. "You know, she's got you both trained quite well."

She took a step forward and felt an unexpected surge of confidence when Brent remained in place, albeit with narrowed eyes. Still, he said nothing.

"I am curious, though." Kayla placed her hands upon his chest. His oh-so-solid chest. "That whole thing about treating me like royalty? Just how far does that extend?"

"I'm the groundskeeper, nothing more."

"Hmm. But you're off the clock now, correct?" Kayla took another step closer, pressing her body lightly into his. "So what do you have planned for after-hours tonight, Mr. Masterson?"

Brent's Adam's apple bobbed. "That depends," he said after a moment, his voice low, rough. "Is this you asking, or the wine?"

Kayla's gaze shifted to his lips. Definitely not the wine, she knew as her pulse quickened. It may have lowered her defenses, but her mind was clear as a bell. A bell that desperately needed a grand distraction. She stretched up on her tiptoes and brought her lips a whisper away from his.

"Me," she breathed. "Definitely me."

His lips parted, but he made no move to kiss her. He was going to turn her down, she realized after a few painfully long seconds. And why not? She'd never tried to seduce a stranger before in her life. Probably looked like a complete idiot, all pressed up against him like this. Besides, just because one hadn't come up in conversation tonight didn't mean he didn't have a girlfriend.

She lowered back down from the balls of her feet and turned toward the door. From the corner of her eye she saw him shift. But instead of reaching past Kayla to open her door and bid her farewell, he stole the clip from her hair. Messy waves tumbled down across her shoulders.

Kayla spun around in surprise. Brent wrapped one hand around her waist while his other slid up the back of her neck to capture a fistful of hair. She sucked in a sharp breath as he gave her hair a not-so-gentle tug, tipping her chin up. The world seemed to grind to a halt as his lips descended upon her exposed neck, then slowly kissed their way to the hollow beneath her ear.

"You want to know my plans?" he asked, his voice a low growl.

Kayla's heart hammered in her ears. "Yes," she managed.

"Then open the door and see for yourself."

Chapter Seven

B rent watched the sunrise Saturday morning from the safety of the Checkerberry's faded red barn, elbows on an open half door and coffee cup in hand. The ice storm was over, its menacing clouds gone. The morning sky looked as if it were on fire, the horizon ablaze in orange and yellow—a subtle reminder of the midnight oil he'd burned with Kayla.

Part of him felt guilty about ever stepping foot inside her suite—it wasn't like him to fraternize with their guests. But how could he when she'd been so easy to please, and so willing to give all he could take? And he'd taken plenty...

He bit back a moan at the memory of her naked body on top of his, blue eyes lit with desire, hair swaying with the rhythm of their hips and skin aglow in the moonlight. Brent had wanted to savor the experience, prolong it, but the urge to devour her was simply too great. And because it'd been forever since he'd been with anyone, he hadn't been able to hold back for long. In fact, it'd been no surprise to him that when Kayla reached her climax, she'd pulled him right along with her.

They had lain beside each other afterward for several minutes in silence, waiting for their heart rates to slow once more. There had been no guilt, no anxiety, only peace—a feeling nearly foreign to Brent these days. *That* he had been able to savor, the moment made even sweeter when her fingers had laced through his.

Eventually, though, Brent had sat up and slid to the edge of the bed. But instead of letting him slip out into the night, what did Kayla do? Wrapped one of those perfect, silky legs around his and flashed him an "I dare you" smile.

Christ, that smile. He was utterly defenseless against it.

The second time around Brent had taken his time, driving her to the brink then backing off time and again. Not to be outdone, Kayla had done the same to him. By the time they each reached the point of no return again, both were utterly spent. They'd collapsed onto the bed, sweaty and sated.

Brent didn't remember falling asleep, but awoke some time later to find his arm draped protectively over her slender body, still innocently curled up beside him. Their embrace felt natural, effortless. Perfect.

That's when he'd made his break for it.

Kayla didn't belong to him or with him. And while she'd given him a night he'd never forget, it was high time he started trying. Happily ever after didn't exist in his world, a fact he'd come to grips with long ago.

"You out here hiding from Ruby's honey-do list, too?"

A smirk tugged at Brent's lips. "No, Miles, you're the one who hides from honey-do lists. They're how I make my living, remember?"

"They're how you *used* to make your living, up until a month ago."

"You come out here to lecture me on how to run my business?"

Miles came to stand beside Brent and propped his elbows on the half door as well. How many times had they stood in this exact spot, drinking coffee, sharing insight? Today, though, Miles seemed more serious than usual as he took a sip of his own coffee, his gaze focused on something off in the distance.

"No. I just hate to see you trade a profitable business for…this."

"She needs my help, Miles."

"What she needs is to retire."

"No." The word came out louder than Brent intended. Somewhere overhead, a startled stowaway bird took flight.

"You think this is what Grandfather would have wanted?" Miles asked. "To watch Ruby work herself to death? And for what? Peanuts?"

"Life isn't just about money."

Miles turned to face Brent. "You're right. Life is about living. And when the shitty economy finally brings this inn to its knees, going under will absolutely kill Ruby. I don't know about you, but that's a sight I don't think I can bear to see."

"Then do something about it. Invest in some advertising, scope out the competition, see what they're doing that we're not."

Miles shook his head, and a lump formed in Brent's throat. Ruby couldn't lose the inn. This place meant everything to her. It was who she was. Hell, it was who they all were. Without it…

"Someone made us an offer."

"An offer to do what?"

"To buy the place."

"Buy it?" Brent looked out over the back lawn, toward the trail that led through the woods and down to the pond. How many summers had he and Miles spent down at that pond? Fishing, canoeing, swimming? He struggled to imagine a reality where that pond wasn't included. "I've never thought about who would run the inn after Ruby."

"Well, they wouldn't necessarily—wait. Look at me."

"Huh?"

Brent's gaze flashed to Miles, whose smirk grew. Shit. Leave it to Miles to read him like a book. Casual as possible, Brent set his coffee down and turned to pick up the nearest tool.

Damn, a broom? That's the best he could do?

"You did it, didn't you?"

"Did what, Miles?"

"Took Kayla to bed last night."

Brent said nothing. Instead, he concentrated his sweeping on a particularly dirty spot on the floor and wished his cousin would let it drop. Which, of course, he wouldn't.

"I'll be damned, you did! Phew. I was beginning to think you'd forfeited your man card. Though I should have put two and two together sooner. You know, after finding you gawking at the pretty sunrise."

"You done yet?"

"Uh oh. Performance issues? Is that why you're out here, instead of still up at the inn?"

Brent resisted the urge to pummel Miles and instead wrapped both hands tightly around the broom handle. "Tell me — when, exactly, did you become such an asshole?"

"Oh, come on, coz. I'm just messing with you. And you gotta admit, I don't get very many opportunities to do that anymore." Miles's face sobered. "So what really happened? Why are you out here, hiding?"

"I'm not hiding," Brent said. "I wanted to get an early start on the day, that's all. Since yesterday was mostly a bust."

"Which might not matter, if Ruby's smart and takes a serious look at this offer. Maybe you could help me convince her to—"

"I'm not going to help you bully her into a decision, Miles. And you'd better not be thinking of doing that, either."

"I'd never bully her, and don't make it sound like I would. But this deal makes solid financial sense for everyone involved."

"That's for Ruby to decide," said Brent. "But until I hear otherwise, I'm going to keep working toward our goal of being ready to open in two weeks. Doesn't leave me much time for—"

"Enjoying yourself?" Miles took another sip of his coffee, then turned and started for the barn's front entrance. "Nah," he muttered. "You're already good at avoiding that all on your own."

Kayla awoke to a pesky beam of sunlight hitting her square in the face. She shifted her surprisingly achy body into a sitting position and looked around, disoriented. The view didn't make any sense to her semi-conscious mind. Pale blue walls. Sheer white drapes, parted. Queen-size bed, sheets in wild disarray.

Sheets. Bed.

Brent.

That explained the whole naked thing. She tugged the nearest sheet over her and shot a look at the space beside her on the bed. Empty.

Kayla lay back and breathed a sigh of relief. There would be no awkward morning after, no need for "thanks, and have a nice life" good-byes. Situations she'd read about, but never experienced herself. She'd never been part of a one-night stand before, let alone initiated one. Her past escapades in the bedroom had been few and far between, but always with someone she'd been dating for some time. Until last night, anyway, when she'd forced herself to just let go.

Kayla's pulse quickened as images of the night before surfaced in her mind. She'd been so worried her limited experience would be obvious, that she'd feel embarrassed and self-conscious. But Brent hadn't made her feel that way at all. Instead, he'd made her feel…beautiful. Desired. Wanted.

And she'd soaked up every second of it. Because, really, when was the last time anyone had made her feel that way? Hmm, that would be never.

She could have stayed in bed all day reliving that memory. Okay, *multiple* memories. Instead, she eventually crawled off the mattress and headed for the shower. It was time to get back to reality, to the real world, where knights in shining armor simply didn't exist.

Nope, in her world, there were only computers and corporate a-holes. One, she could unplug and walk away from. The other? Well, if they thought she was going to tuck her tail and run, they had another thing coming. Because after the night Kayla just had, she felt ready to take on the world. Even, perhaps, the untouchable Joe Freimann.

Forty-five minutes later, she headed downstairs, refreshed and eager to get on the road. At the bottom landing, Kayla paused to listen. Silence. Relief washed over her anew.

But a different emotion battled for her attention as she stepped toward the dining room: disappointment. She brushed off the feeling and silently scolded herself. Seeing Brent would only complicate things. And probably get her all hot and bothered, which would be entirely counterproductive. This was much better, she told herself. No messy good-byes, no strings attached.

"Good morning, dear. Did you sleep well?" Ruby called from behind the bar top by the kitchen entrance. Her face was as bright and cheery as ever, free of suspicion as to what might have transpired between Kayla and her grandson in the night.

Kayla breathed another mental sigh of relief. Silly as it may be, she didn't want to leave that type of impression on her gracious hostess. Especially since she'd never dreamed of having a fling before. Ever. Good girls like her just didn't do that type of thing. She slid into a seat at the bar and pushed her oncoming guilt trip aside.

"Slept like a rock, and I don't usually sleep well when I'm away from home. Had to have been that amazing bed. If I had a bigger car I'd try to smuggle it back home with me. I've never slept better."

Kayla clamped her mouth shut. She was rambling, a sure sign of guilt. Thankfully, Ruby appeared unfazed by it.

"I'm so glad to hear that. We upgraded all our beds a

few years back, after Miles read about a direct correlation between comfort and satisfaction in some study on successful hotel chains. All those statistics and what not are just stuff and nonsense to me. But Miles? He eats it up."

She poured Kayla a cup of coffee, then brought over a little caddy holding dainty containers of cream and sugar. "Hungry, dear? I've still got plenty of pancake batter in the back, and some bacon. I could even make up some eggs. Or fruit, perhaps?"

"I don't know, it all sounds so good." Kayla laughed. "Guess I'm just not used to having more than cold cereal as a breakfast option."

"It's no wonder you're skinny as a rail. People should eat real food for breakfast, not something out of a box."

"You know, bacon and eggs do sound pretty good." Kayla peered at the wall clock across the room. "I'm just not sure how long I have until the tow truck arrives, though. Have they called yet?"

"No, the phone has been quiet all morning. Which means we should have plenty of time to get some food in your stomach. How do you like your eggs, dear?"

"Um, scrambled would be great, thank you."

Kayla waited for Ruby to disappear behind the kitchen door before allowing her shoulders to slump with disappointment. She was itching to get on the road, to get home and start plotting her revenge. There had to be something she could do to get back at Joe for setting her up. But what? And could she do it without burning what was left of the smoldering bridge between her and her boss?

Before she could come up with a suitable ploy, the kitchen door swung open again. Ruby stepped out, a heaping plate of bacon and eggs in her hand.

"Oh, thank you, it looks amazing. But you made so much."

"Just do your best, sweetheart. Wouldn't want to send you off still hungry."

Kayla took those words to heart and began to devour her breakfast. After the night she'd had, it was no wonder she was starving. Had bacon and eggs ever tasted so good? She glanced up in Ruby's direction when she paused to take a drink of her coffee, and was surprised to see the older woman frowning down at the clipboard before her.

"Everything all right, Ruby?" Kayla asked.

"Oh, yes. Just so much left to do before we open for the season. I'm usually further along in our preparations by now, but we've had some issues come up unexpectedly that set us back a bit." She waved off the list and came over to refill Kayla's coffee mug. "Nothing we can't handle, I'm sure."

"Does it take a lot of people to run a place like this?"

"Not really. For the longest time it was just John and me. Our children had grown and moved off." Ruby looked across the dining room toward the sun streaming in through the nearest window and smiled. "John always said he bought me the inn because he knew I needed something to take care of. I would have settled for a puppy in those days, but he joked that we wouldn't have to housebreak an inn. Though there have been times when the inn nearly broke us."

Her smile dimmed momentarily then brightened once more. "Business really picked up in the nineties, though, so we brought on a groundskeeper. Then a cleaning gal. When Miles finished college, he volunteered to oversee my financ-es. Truthfully, I think he's after his inheritance." Ruby leaned in close with a devilish grin on her face and winked. "Too bad I'm planning on spending every last cent myself."

Kayla couldn't help but laugh.

"These past few years he's done a fine job of spending it for me, though," Ruby continued. "New beds. New dishes. New paint. New landscaping. The boy's run me ragged. And then he comes up with this cockamamie idea to bring in a chef—a chef! Whatever was wrong with my cooking, I asked."

"What did he say?"

"That I work too hard." Ruby scowled. "And that bringing in someone with the title of 'chef' would boost our occupancy rates. Bah! Titles and rates are for number crunchers, not innkeepers. Let me cook my own darned food."

"Well, I, for one, think your cooking is amazing."

"Thank you, dear." Ruby sighed. "To be honest, though, Maddie is much better than I ever was when it comes to presentation. She has a way with all those artsy-fartsy sauce decorations. I suppose if that's what people want—"

"Then that's what we'll give them," said Miles, strolling in from the lobby. "We aim to please. Speaking of which, Kayla, your tow truck just arrived."

"Oh."

She met Ruby's gaze and watched as the spark in the innkeeper's eyes dimmed. Or more likely, Kayla imagined it did. Ruby had hundreds, if not thousands, of guests, and she was just the latest one. And now, whether Kayla wanted it to be or not, playtime was over. Ruby had an inn to run. Kayla had a career to salvage, rent to pay, and a man who'd gifted her one amazing night to try and forget.

"Great, thank you." She slid out of her seat and forced a smile onto her face. "I'll go and get my things."

Brent lowered the arm of his miter saw and watched another sliver float to the ground from a tricky piece of crown molding. God, he loved his DeWalt. Two years old and this baby still cut like a hot knife through butter.

"You can come out now," Miles called from the doorway. "It's safe again."

Brent pushed his safety glasses up off his face and threw an annoyed look at his cousin. "Safe to do what?"

"Leave the barn. Tow truck just left, she's gone now."

Brent worked to keep his face neutral. He'd prepared himself all morning, knew it was for the best that she go. So why did he feel like someone had just knocked the wind out of him?

Nice job, you idiot. You stood back and let your one bright spot in an otherwise dreary existence walk right out the door.

He crossed the room and selected another piece of crown molding from the uncut stack. "Good. So now that you no longer have to worry about keeping up appearances, you ready to start helping me?"

"I'll have you know I was working inside, not socializing. Just because mine takes place behind a computer screen doesn't mean it's not work."

"If you say so." Brent leveled a grin at his cousin.

"Oh, great. You go and get laid for the first time in decades and now I get to suffer through your good mood?"

"And that's any worse than suffering through my bad moods?"

"Good point. By the way, I swung by your house on my way back from town, fed your pooch."

"Thanks."

"Yeah, you owe me now." Miles picked up a can of primer. "She still insisting on white?"

She?

Oh. Ruby. Brent ran a hand over the back of his neck. Best to hurry up and get the other "she" out of his head before he went and said something stupid in front of Miles.

"Yeah. And as much as I hate to admit, it's gonna look sharp against those pale lilac walls. Will be a bitch to keep clean, though."

"As long as neither of us has to clean it, I don't really care."

"Then you'd better hope the cleaning woman Ruby lined up doesn't quit on her, too. Oh, and you might want to bump up Maddie's grocery allowance."

Miles pried the primer's lid open and threw Brent a quizzical look. "What does our chef's budget have to do with housekeeping?"

"Everything. If you want to fill this place, you need to give people a reason to come here. Maddie's one hell of a cook— we need to talk her up, advertise her menus or something. She could really put the Checkerberry back on the map."

Miles just shrugged, his gaze intent on the paint he was stirring. It wasn't like him to back off from an argument, no matter how small or irrelevant. And when he changed the topic to baseball, Brent knew something was up. Because Miles never instigated a conversation about baseball the day after his Yanks lost.

Great. As if trying to get Kayla off his mind wasn't worry enough.

Chapter Eight

Kayla lay on the tattered, hand-me-down couch wedged into a corner of the tiny mezzanine at Smithson Motors, staring up at the auto repair shop's ceiling joists. She hated that she'd had to call her father with the news she wouldn't be by to see him today. After spending so much of her energy trying to take stress off of him, the last thing she wanted to do was add to it. Which is why she was in the midst of telling one doozy of a lie.

But hey, what he didn't know couldn't hurt him. Right?

"So you went up to see Tommy on Friday, without checking the weather first?" he asked, doubt clear in his voice. Understandable, since she had made a habit of giving him the five-day forecast every time they spoke. And the one for the weekend. And maybe the extended forecast, too.

"Yeah, I guess I was just so surprised to be" — *punished* — "granted some time off that I didn't bother to check. Heck, it's been so long since I took a vacation I guess I forgot how to do it." She laughed, and hoped like mad her father couldn't hear the hollowness in the sound as well as she could.

"Well, I'm relieved to hear you didn't have to drive in that freezing rain. It was all over the news Friday, accidents everywhere. Roads can turn slick without a moment's notice in freak storms like that."

Tell me about it. "No worries, I'm safe and sound here with Tommy. We're just kicking back, hanging out, like the old days."

Her gaze shifted to the shop's dark office. Oh, how she wished Tommy *was* here to keep her company. He and Pixie Cut had yet to return from their trip to Windsor, and she'd been lonely as all get out with them gone. Of course, she'd had no intention of remaining in Mount Pleasant once the tow truck picked her up yesterday. But Jimmy had taken one look at her Impala's front end after hoisting it out of the ditch and deemed her baby undrivable. Neither of them had been able to reach Tommy, so Jimmy made the executive decision to bring both Kayla and her car back to Smithson Motors—the shop her brother co-owned with Rex Smithson.

With her car out of commission, she'd spent the last twenty-four hours rotating between moping and brainstorming ways to get back in her boss's good graces. But without a decent wifi connection, her progress had been rather limited. Sure, she could have checked in to a nearby chain hotel, but God-only-knew how much she was looking at in car repairs, and money was already tight. And while she knew from the placard in her room at the Checkerberry that they had wifi there, no way was Kayla going to go back and ask Ruby to grant her another free night's stay.

No, to do that would only make things worse. She'd

managed to make a clean break from the inn with its kindly owner and her surprisingly agile and eager to please handyman grandson. And as much as being away from them for only a few hours had bothered her, she had a feeling it'd be a heck of a lot harder to walk away from the Mastersons and their cozy Checkerberry a second time.

"I'm so thankful that you and your brother have stayed close over the years, sweetheart. After your mother passed, well, I worried everyone would go their separate ways. She was always the glue that held our family together."

The sincerity in his voice nearly drove her to tears. "We're not going anywhere, Dad," she promised quietly.

"You might not be, but Tommy's as good as a Michigander now that he's co-owner of that shop. I'm so damned proud of that boy."

"Me, too." Pride swelled in her heart as well. But unfortunately, her father was right. With Tommy out of state, that left Kayla to keep watch over their father. It didn't matter that he was only in his early fifties, she planned to watch him like a hawk. After all, cancer had stolen her mother at an even younger age.

Her phone beeped in her ear. "Hang on, I'm getting another call."

A quick glance showed it was the call she'd been waiting for all weekend. She checked the time: quarter to eleven. *About darned time, little brother.*

"Sorry, Dad, I need to take this. It's Tommy."

"Tommy? I thought you said you were there with him?"

Kayla froze, wide-eyed. Oh, God. She stank at lying, always had. And her father was the king of sniffing out lies.

"I am," she said, digging the hole deeper. "But he

stepped out a few minutes ago to grab us some breakfast from a place down the street. Must have forgotten what I asked for."

"Breakfast? At almost eleven?"

"Love you, Daddy. Remember to take your cholesterol medicine, and I'll call tomorrow, okay?"

"All right. I will. Love you, too, sweetheart. Tell your brother the same."

"Will do." She clicked to switch calls and took a deep breath. "Tommy?"

"Morning, Sis. Saw I'd missed a few of your calls—sorry about that. Did Jimmy get you all taken care of?"

"Not exactly."

Her gaze panned out across the auto repair shop's main floor. Rex Smithson had been looking for an apprentice to train and eventually be his successor. Tommy had been Rex's perfect diamond in the rough, and not only helped bring in a steady stream of business from his college buddies but also helped to fix the place up. Still, it was a far cry from her suite at the Checkerberry Inn.

"What do you mean, not exactly?" Tommy asked.

"Well, he couldn't get there until yesterday."

"Aw nuts, really? I'm sorry, Kay. He usually makes good on his promises."

"I'm sure it wasn't his fault. The roads were awful, and he had other jobs in front of mine. Guess it was good Brent found me, since his grandmother owns a bed-and-breakfast and all."

A scene involving tangled sheets and soft moonlight entered her thoughts. Kayla couldn't help but grin as she remembered worrying when he first pulled alongside her on the road that *he* might try to take advantage of *her*.

"God, I hope that place didn't cost you an arm and a leg. I've driven by there before, looks pretty fancy. Or at least, like it used to."

"Actually, it didn't cost me a dime. The innkeeper felt so bad for me, she wouldn't let me pay."

"Sweet. You didn't have to wait too long for Jimmy to show up on Saturday, did you?"

"No, not too long."

"Awesome. I worried about you all night Friday. Heather kept telling me you'd be fine, but I had this feeling something wasn't right. Probably why I lost my shirt on Let It Ride. Oh, well, it was just good to get away for a few days, you know?"

Kayla smirked. "Yeah, I do."

"So, was Jacober camped out on your doorstep, waiting for you to come home so he could beg you to come back?"

"I wouldn't know, I haven't been there yet."

There was a short pause. "What?"

"I never made it home, all right? When Jimmy and I got to the Impala, he said no way could I drive it. Something about front subframe damage. All I saw was a slightly crumpled bumper." She scowled out across the shop floor at her battered car. *Stupid ice storm.*

"So what'd he do?"

"Towed the car to the only shop in town that wasn't jam-packed with wrecks from the night before."

"Which one was that?"

"Yours."

Tommy chuckled. "Well, at least you know you'll get a fair price. I'll take a look at it as soon as I'm back. In fact, I can swing by and pick you up on my way. You did find someplace to stay last night, didn't you?"

"Sure did. Though, I gotta tell ya—this couch you and Rex picked up? Yeah, not as comfy as it looks."

"Please tell me you're joking, Kay."

"What? It's not so bad, once you get used to the smell of oil and stuff."

He cursed under his breath. "You're nuts, you know that? Staying there with the heat turned down. Hell, I think Rex even said something about a mouse last week."

"Oh yeah, definitely one running around. Mickey and I got acquainted last night." A little too well, actually. The shop's tiny bathroom definitely wasn't big enough for the two of them. Made it harder to fall asleep, too, not knowing where the furry little beast had scurried off to after her introductory shrieks. "But hey, I survived. And when it got chilly in here I bumped up the thermostat a tad. Hope you don't mind."

"Mind? No, what I mind is that my sister was stuck sleeping on our shitty couch last night. Why didn't you just go back to the Check—?"

"The couch was fine," she lied. "But if you feel that bad about it, you can make it up to me by getting back and fixing my car so I can be on my way. Honestly, I like Mount Pleasant and all, but the thought of being home and in my own bed has never sounded better."

Even if Brent isn't in it waiting for me. Though that would make it a whole lot more fun to come home to…

Kayla gave herself another mental slap.

"We're about an hour out yet, but I'll drop Heather off at her place and then head straight to the shop. But, Kay, I can't promise anything without seeing the Impala."

Panic seeped into Kayla's chest. She couldn't stay in Mount Pleasant another day. There was cleaning to do at home. Shopping to be done, redemption to be gained. "No promises? But you're the world's best mechanic."

"Yeah, well, the world's best mechanic doesn't exactly have spare Impala subframe parts laying around his shop."

She swallowed hard. "Can't you just...buy them from one of the other shops in town?"

"No idea if anyone else has them, or has them and hasn't already committed them to their own jobs. Look, sit tight and we'll get something figured out, okay?"

In a fog of disappointment, Kayla thanked her brother, hung up, and tried to ignore the sinking feeling that it may be a while before she'd see Indiana again. A long while. She hoped like crazy that wouldn't be the case. Because the sooner she could get back, the sooner she could stop lying to her father about being stuck here. Or why she'd skipped town in the first place.

B rent collected his tools from the Gooseberry Suite Sunday evening and tried to compile a mental checklist of everything he had left to do before the Checkerberry opened. But his mind refused to cooperate. Instead, it kept shifting back to a certain someone he'd sworn he would be able to love, leave, and forget.

So far, he hadn't had any luck with that last part.

He'd tried to stay busy Saturday, cutting, priming, and painting crown molding in the barn until well past dark. Miles had stuck around for no more than a few hours, which left the rest of Brent's day much too susceptible to daydreaming. Which totally sucked, since he kept picturing Kayla's peaches and cream skin under him. And over him. And on him.

Sheer torture is what it was.

That's why he'd kept working. If he had to concentrate on an important task like not losing a few fingers to the saw, then he somehow managed to keep her off his mind. But as soon as he'd start a mindless task like stirring paint, those damned images would creep right back in.

When his strength had finally given out, Brent headed for the inn. He'd been unwilling to go home, to face a lonely house and cold bed. Instead, he climbed the rear staircase up to the second floor, made his way into the Strawberry Suite, and promptly collapsed onto the bed he should have slept in Friday night. After a quick text to Miles asking his cousin to check on his assuredly lonely pooch one more time, Brent fell fast asleep.

Damn it, how could one night with a perfect stranger have managed to slice through his emotional barriers? Before, he'd been utterly convinced he could survive on his own. Could live the rest of his days just me, myself, and I. But then Kayla had walked into EAT and turned that thinking on its head.

And a small part of him hated her for it.

The next morning at breakfast, Ruby didn't question his decision to stay. In fact, for the first time in ages she didn't even try to pry into his closed thoughts. Maybe the misery was plain enough on his face, or maybe it was because she seemed preoccupied with her clipboard of honey-dos. Either way, the dining room felt empty without Kayla, and that realization steered him from the table and right back out to the barn once the meal was over and plates had been cleared.

After a full morning of painting today, all Brent had left to do inside was hang the molding—a task he dragged out as long as possible. Unfortunately, even with Miles interrupting to "help" a few times, Brent finished just after six o'clock. With a sigh, he headed downstairs and out to his truck, determined to man up and face reality.

Your grandmother really does rule the roost, doesn't she?

Brent scowled at the memory of Kayla's taunting as he drove and did his damnedest to block the images that were sure to follow. Thankfully, the moment he stepped foot inside his back door, an overgrown ball of fur slammed into him and demanded his full attention.

"Miss me, boy?" he asked, dodging his pup's wet, slobbery kisses. "Oh, come on, now. I was only gone for a weekend."

Though his four-legged roommate was used to Brent working dawn to dusk, it was rare his owner ever stayed away for an entire night. Even so, Brent couldn't help but think for the hundredth time that the enclosed dog run, which extended off the back porch, was worth its weight in gold. It kept him from being burdened with guilt if he worked too long.

Once kibble and water bowls had been refilled, Brent ignored an angry snarl from his own stomach and headed upstairs. Food could wait. What he needed was to wash a day's worth of paint and sawdust off his weary body.

Melancholy filled him as he made his way down the main hallway and up the creaky old staircase. It had never been

Brent's intention to settle down in Mount Pleasant—he'd always dreamed of leaving the small town behind, of chasing his own dreams to somewhere warmer. But when his parents died, their home, filled with their memories, their scents, and their history, was all he had left. Usually he found comfort in his solitude, strength in these familiar surroundings. Tonight, loneliness was all the quiet old farmhouse had to offer him.

Nothing a hot shower and some HGTV couldn't fix.

No sooner had he reached the top step than his cell phone rang. A long sigh escaped him as he spied Miles's number on its display.

"What?"

"Hey, coz. Whatcha doin'?"

Miles's voice was loud, the background noise only slightly lesser so. Brent pinched the bridge of his nose. *Please don't need me to bail you out of anything tonight...* "Getting ready to jump in the shower. Why?"

"You're just now getting cleaned up? I left you hours ago."

Brent reached his room and swiped a pair of clean boxer briefs from his top dresser drawer. "Yeah, I know. Took me all afternoon to fix your work."

"Whatever. You eaten yet?"

Brent's stomach rumbled in answer, the sound followed this time by a stabbing pain. Not enough pain to risk admitting his hunger. Lord only knew why Miles was even asking. "Not hungry."

"Liar. You're always hungry; you just forget to eat."

He sighed. Miles knew Brent all too well, as he should—they'd been nearly inseparable as kids. Growing up out in the country, away from downtown Mount Pleasant, there weren't a lot of other options. And while the boys had their differences and went on to make new friends in high school and college, they'd stayed close.

When fate stole Brent's parents, his friends had tried to comfort him, to boost his spirits. Over time, all but Miles grew tired of his new unsociable ways and moved on. When Miles's parents moved to Nebraska a year later, he stayed behind to oversee the finances at the Checkerberry Inn. He also maintained his role as relentless wingman for one for-ever-jaded Brent Masterson.

A role that, well-intentioned or not, often drove Brent to near insanity.

"What do you want, Miles?"

"Remember that cute blonde I said I was meeting up with tonight over at Chevvy's? Well, she brought a friend. A *lonely* friend. And you know how I can't stand to see anyone be alone."

Brent snorted. "Is she hot?"

"Give me some credit, B. Would I set you up with anything less?"

Wouldn't be the first time. "Is she wet?"

"Wow, one night in the sack sure stoked your appetite."

"And made of porcelain?"

There was a pause on the other end. "Well, she's not an albino, if that's what you mean."

"What I mean," Brent said, cranking on the hot water in his bathroom, "is I want a shower tonight, nothing more. I appreciate you looking out for the lonely blonde and all, but I—"

"Come *on*, man. Don't do this."

"Don't do what?"

"Have one great night with someone and then close yourself back off to the rest of the world. We miss the old Brent." He lowered his voice. "I miss you."

"Aw, you're warming my heart." *And making me feel like a complete asshole.*

"You owe me," Miles insisted. "I checked on your dog twice yesterday, remember?"

"Yes. And as memory serves, you still owe me way more than I owe you."

"Would it sweeten the deal if I mentioned your little one-night stand is here, too?"

Brent froze. Kayla was still in town?

It couldn't be her. She had a job back in Indiana, one she seemed to love, judging by the way she yacked everyone's ear off about it at dinner the other night. Maybe she'd stayed a little longer to visit with her brother?

No, no maybes, and no Kayla. Miles was just trying to get him out of the house, and Brent wasn't falling for it.

"Wow, man, you must really be desperate for my company because that's low, even for you."

"I don't do desperate, and I'm not blowing smoke. She's here."

Damn. Miles sure didn't sound like he was lying. And the guy was one sorry-ass bluffer. But so what if she was still in town, Brent wondered as he tugged his shirt off. It wasn't like she'd want to see him again. They'd shared a night together, then gone their separate ways. Clearly, she was fine with that, since she hadn't bothered to say anything to him before she left on Saturday.

Then again, he hadn't really given her a chance to.

Brent stood, listening to his limited supply of hot water

run down the drain and weighed his options: go and see for himself if she was there, or stay home and try not to think about how he'd blown the chance to catch one last glimpse of those blue eyes and hourglass figure. Because, whether she was there or not, he knew it would be the last time. Kayla had Indiana, and that's where he wanted her to be. It was better that way.

Still, sneaking one last peek at her couldn't hurt any…

"Where're you at?"

"Chevvy's. Just promise not to spend your whole date gawking at Kayla, all right?"

"Fine. Give me twenty minutes. And order me the usual."

Chapter Nine

*M*id-state Suicide. *Gamble-Your-Bowels Spicy Garlic. Campus Curry.* Kayla set the wings menu down and threw her brother a skeptical look. A look he didn't see, as he was lip-locked with his pixie-haired girlfriend. Again.

All that huggy-bear, kissy-face nonsense was putting a serious damper on Kayla's appetite. And since the repair parts for her car wouldn't even arrive until mid-week, her time as captive audience was just beginning. Yay...

"Does this place offer any sauce that doesn't threaten to kill you?"

Tommy drew back from Heather and grinned. "Yeah, the milder options are on the other side. But I thought you liked hot and spicy."

Hot and spicy is what I had at the Checkerberry.

The memory of Friday night instantly jabbed at her lonely heart. From night of passion to playing second fiddle to her brother's love interest. Oh, how far she'd fallen.

"Yeah, I'm kinda feeling like keeping it mild tonight."

"Then you should go with the teriyaki boneless wings. If you get a basket, there'll be a ton of fries, too," Tommy said.

She nodded, then glanced over at Heather, who was busy studying her cuticles. Kayla wanted to like the girl, really she did. Too bad the feeling didn't appear to be mutual. "So, Heather, what do you usually get here?"

"Me?" Heather looked up, boredom written all over her face. "Oh, just a salad. Gotta watch my weight—I'm auditioning for a show next week that calls for a tall, thin waitress."

"That's why she's been working at EAT," Tommy chimed in. "To train for her role, you know?"

"Oh. Cool."

Pride laced her brother's voice and shone in his eyes. Clearly, he was smitten with Pixie Cut. Kayla snuck another glance at her, trying to figure out why, but came up empty. Sure, the chick was cute, but she seemed a little lacking in personality. And low on the friendliness meter, too. Kayla went back to hiding behind her menu.

"So?" Tommy asked.

She looked up, confused. "So, what?"

"So, didn't she seem like a natural at the diner on Friday? I think she's a shoo-in for the part."

"Aw, you really think so, pooky?" asked Heather.

"Uh-huh."

Okay, she could handle a kiss or two. But when they went and got all starry-eyed and started in with baby names, that was where Kayla drew the line. She grabbed the wallet from her purse and slid out of her seat.

"I think I'm gonna hit the bar, get a beer after all. You

two want me to grab you anything while I'm up?"

"No thanks, Kay."

"Good," she muttered once she was out of earshot. A quick glance back found them murmuring God only knows what into each other's ears. Bleck. Kayla would never dream of hanging all over someone in public like that. Then again, she'd never been with anyone who made her want to.

Except Brent.

She'd considered looking for him Saturday morning before the tow truck arrived, but had no clue where to begin. And besides—if he really wanted to see her, he would have sought her out. Apparently, he was a one-night stand kind of guy. Which, honestly, was all she could afford to give him. Her life was cemented in place three hours south of here.

But even aside from her night of passion with Brent, she'd loved it at the Checkerberry Inn. Spending time there with Ruby and the guys had been the closest thing to a sense of home she'd felt since…well, since her mother had passed.

Kayla swallowed hard and pushed an all-too-familiar ache aside as she wove through the smattering of tables that cluttered the bar. According to Tommy, the building was an old barn restored by some guy who belonged to a local bike gang. So while the patrons could be a bit scary at times, the food was to die for.

She glanced up at the second floor, which was wide open in the center. Railings kept the diners upstairs tucked safely away, but allowed for an open view of the bar and floor below. A vaguely familiar-looking man and two bleach-blondes sat at a table across the room from where Kayla stood. She scoffed at the idea of anyone looking familiar, since the only people she knew in town were—

Wait, was that…*Miles*?

Distracted, she didn't see the man ahead of her backing away from the bar with a fresh beer at his lips. Her foot connected with his just before their bodies collided.

"What the hell?"

Kayla's gaze flashed to the leather-clad biker looming before her. He was a moose of a man with beady black eyes and a zigzagging scar that ran from the corner of one eyebrow down to his cheekbone. His goatee was graying and overgrown but did little to hide the sneer on his face as his gaze raked over her. Darn it, she knew wearing the yoga pants, fitted exercise top, and sneakers she'd dug out of the gym bag in her back seat had been a bad idea. Then again, her corporate attire would have made her stick out even more.

"You lost or something, little girl?" he asked, wiping spilled beer from his chin. "This ain't no kiddy bar."

"Sorry. Guess I wasn't looking where I was going."

She offered him an apologetic look and tried to step around him, but the big lug blocked her path.

"Oh, I can take you where you want to go, baby," he said, leaning in closer.

The beer could wait, she decided, and took a step back. But another body stopped her progress. Kayla turned and found herself staring up at a tall, thick woman cracking her knuckles.

"What the hell are you doing trying to pick up my man, you little hussy?"

B rent pulled into the packed lot at Chevvy's and frowned. Didn't all these people have something better to do on a Sunday night than drink? Hell, didn't he have better things to do? Like wake up from this crazy idea that catching one last look at Kayla from across a crowded bar might somehow make his day better?

Deep down he knew the mere sight of her was going to be like pouring salt on a fresh wound. But the fear of missing out on his last chance to see her before she disappeared from his life forever had driven him here. It both amazed and infuriated him that one night had left him so vulnerable. Brent wasn't the type to get hung up on a woman. Not since Nikki, anyway…

He shook his head and pushed past hurts aside. Time to man up. Go in, eat some wings, catch a fleeting glimpse of Kayla, play nice with Miles and his harem, and then leave. Alone. Without the woman Miles had waiting for him upstairs, and definitely without Kayla.

Brent backed the truck into a far spot on the old barn's overflow lot and peeled off the Masterson Construction logo magnets on the cab doors. He had a clean reputation to uphold, after all. Though now that he was working for Ruby, who knew how much of his own business he'd have time for anymore? Too bad Miles wasn't worth a damn when it came to anything construction-related. Computers and women he could do. Wield a hammer or nail gun? Not so much.

The sign above the bar's back entrance welcomed tonight's musical guest: The Brotherhood. Brent stopped in his tracks and cursed. The Brotherhood? Really?

Any other band would have been fine with him. Hell, they could have had dueling cellos onstage tonight for all he cared. But The Brotherhood? He wondered if their latest lead singer was as much a girlfriend-stealing dirtbag as the infamous Derek Stringer had been.

If Karma truly did exist, Nikki had run out on that arrogant bastard by now, too.

Brent forced his feet forward once more and pulled the back door open. Shouting, laughter, and catcalls spilled out to meet him. *Damn redneck biker bar.* If Chevvy's didn't serve the best wings around, he'd never come here. Too bad he and Miles both had a thing for wings.

He'd no sooner spotted Miles sitting with two bleach-blondes at a table upstairs than shouts erupted near the bar. Brent turned to see some tall, black-leather-clad heavy woman going off about God only knows what. *Guess tonight the bar's serving dinner and a show*, he thought with an eye roll. Hopefully she was all bark and no bite—nothing ruined a meal like police interrogations and eyewitness testimonies.

Unfortunately, that wasn't to be. Three steps up the stair-case, Brent glanced back to see Noisy's fist rocket forward. The person before her bobbed out of the way, and the punch connected instead with Butch, an aging, behemoth of a man who was a regular at Chevvy's. A howl of rage rang out, and heads all around the bar turned. Those closest to the out-burst stepped back, providing Brent with a clear view of the person who had dodged the blow—a small, slender brunette dressed in a cheery jogging outfit.

Oh, please God, no.

He squinted and studied the brunette. Sure enough, it was Kayla. *Of course it is*, he thought as he tore back down the steps and began elbowing his way through the masses. The woman seemed to have a bad luck streak a mile long.

"Stop movin', dammit," yelled Noisy. "You dumb enough to hit on my man, then you're gonna have to deal with me."

"Really, this was all just a big misunderstanding," Kayla cried.

"Oh, you got that right."

Brent reached the inner circle of spectators just as the woman pulled her arm back to throw another punch. She proved to be an even bigger girl up close—he'd have to tackle her to keep her from beating Kayla to a pulp. But if he did that, Butch would kill him for sure.

He looked around, frantic for another option. A young member of their bike gang stood to his left, shouting words of encouragement to Noisy, and something inside Brent snapped. He charged forward and plowed a shoulder into the punk with all he had, then ducked back into the crowd for cover. The kid barreled forward and fell into Noisy's left side just as her fist propelled forward once more. The collision knocked them both off-balance, and the two tumbled to the floor in a flailing heap.

As the crowd leaned forward to get a better look at the mass of tangled bodies, Brent wove his way over to Kayla. He snagged her arm and gave it a solid jerk away from the mayhem. With a startled squeak she turned to see who'd grabbed her.

"Brent!"

"We gotta move." He pushed her ahead of him and snuck a quick look back. Butch had the punk by his shirt. The kid was pleading his case, his eyes frantically scanning the crowd for the true culprit. Their window of opportunity for a clean escape was narrowing fast.

The punk's gaze landed on him. *Shit.*

"Faster, Kayla." He gave her another shove.

"To where?"

"The back door. Up ahead." The crowd was thinner on this side of the bar. Good for speed, bad for cover. No time to worry, though. They'd just have to take their chances. "My truck's two rows over. No matter what, keep going. You've got to get out—"

A hand the size of a bear's paw snagged his bicep. Brent turned to see one of Butch's cronies staring down at him, a wicked grin on his face.

"Where do you think you're going?"

A chorus broke out behind Kayla as she neared the back door.

"Fight! Fight! Fight! Fight!"

She looked back and froze. The arm of one seriously big—and seriously scary—biker was pulling Brent back toward the mayhem. She had to help him, but how?

"Just go!" he yelled as he struggled to twist free from the other guy's grip.

"But—"

"*Go!*"

A flying bottle of beer crashed into the wall beside her. Good God, what kind of place was this? With a scream she bolted outside.

The door slammed shut behind her, echoing like a thunderclap across the parking lot. Ignoring the sting of crisp spring air against her skin, she raced away from the bar and its muffled pounding music, angry shouts, and sounds of continuing destruction. Truck. She'd get to his truck, hope like heck it was unlocked, and then call the cops. Surely they'd help her save Brent.

But as she raced down the second row of vehicles past the old barn, panic threatened to consume her. There wasn't a *single* black Silverado in sight—there were *dozens*. And none had his Masterson logo on the side. Crap! Where the heck had he parked?

She'd zipped through every row anywhere near the exit and was just circling around for a second pass when the back door slammed open and shut. Brent shot out like a bullet and disappeared into the darkness. A few seconds later, a truck two rows over *boop-booped* as its headlights came to life.

"Kayla?" he cried.

Relief washed over her as she took off in that direction. "Coming!"

The back door slammed open again, sending another loud *crack!* across the dark lot. The oversized biker guy burst outside. He stopped and scanned the sea of vehicles, a line of bright red blood trickling down from a cut above his right eye. Kayla darted off the main aisle and began picking her way through the dark toward Brent's truck.

"Coward! Get back here and fight like a m—"

Brent's truck roared to life, drowning out the guy's taunting. Kayla dashed across the last gap between her and Brent's truck and sprinted toward it with all she had left. The passenger side door hung open. With the last of her energy, she dove inside.

"'Bout damn time," Brent growled. "Hang on."

The truck surged forward, and Kayla scrambled to pull the door shut before she toppled right back out. Brent veered away from the building and started through the maze of vehicles that sat between them and the main road. Kayla spun to face backward and hung on for dear life as the truck bobbed and wove through the lot. They were nearly to the main road when she saw the scary biker woman emerge from the bar, a broken beer bottle held high in her hand, its jagged edge pointed in their direction.

"That woman's crazy!"

"Too bad you didn't figure that out before you pissed her off."

"I didn't mean to. It was all just a big misunderstanding."

"Well, your big misunderstanding might have earned me a few broken knuckles," Brent said, grimacing as he curled and uncurled his left hand.

"I am so, so sorry." She turned in her seat and ran a shaky hand through her hair. "All I wanted was to spend a nice, quiet evening with my brother." Her eyes widened. "Oh my gosh! Tommy! He's got to be worried sick about me."

"Well, call him and let him know you're okay. I'll drive you back to—"

A chorus of motorcycle engines roared to life behind them. Brent's gaze flashed to the rearview mirror.

"Damn. Looks like we're not out of the woods, yet."

Kayla twisted in her seat to sneak a glance out the truck's back window. A swarm of headlights was funneling out of Chevvy's lot. "Oh my God. Should we call the police or something?"

"No time for that," he said, squinting out into the darkness before them.

"But we can't outrun them in this thing!"

"Not on the main road, I can't. Now where is that damn…

ah, there it is." He threw her a devious grin. "You'd better buckle up, princess. The ride's about to get a little bumpy."

Kayla scrambled to latch her belt. "Bumpy?"

Brent cranked the wheel hard right. An *oof!* escaped her as the seat belt constricted around her chest. The truck skidded off the road and down a steep embankment.

"Are you trying to get us *killed*?"

"No, I'm trying to save our necks. Do you trust me?"

The truck leveled out and tore off through a farmer's recently tilled field. Even with her seat belt fastened, Kayla bounced like a ragdoll in the seat beside him.

"D-d-d-o I-I h-a-a-a-ve a ch-ch-ch-ch-oice?" she cried.

The truck eventually came to a dirt access road, and the rough ride went from whiplash-inducing to merely teeth-rattling. Kayla twisted in her seat and hung onto its edge to get a look out the rear window. The band of bikers had congregated back on the main road around where the Silverado had started its unexpected detour. One headlight trickled down off the road and into the field behind them. Then another.

"Brent…"

"Yeah, I see 'em."

Kayla felt the truck slow to a stop.

"Damn," Brent mumbled. "The creek's higher than I expected."

Her gaze flashed forward. Sure enough, a wide creek wound its way through the dark field ahead of them, its contents glittering beneath the moonlight like a giant mystic snake. "Is that a bad thing?"

The devious grin returned to his face.

"Only if we get stuck," he said, and stepped on the gas.

Chapter Ten

Brent stepped out of his truck and slammed the door behind him.

Why? Why had he felt the need to rescue this damned woman again? Granted, he'd gotten one hell of an adrenaline rush from the fight and the escape. But now he had a throbbing left hand and a wanted woman in his truck. A single woman. A sexy, single woman. Whom he'd seen naked… from just about every angle possible.

He looked back to the cab and discovered Kayla had made no move to exit the vehicle. Either all that bouncing around had jarred loose something inside her, or she was still trying to get over her fright from the bar. Brent wanted to comfort her, to calm her down, but could he do those things and still manage to keep his heart safe?

He ran his good hand through his hair and took a deep breath. *Get it together, man.* It wasn't like she would fall in love with the country atmosphere and beg to never go home.

He'd be polite, invite her in, and keep a safe distance. The coast would be clear in an hour or two. Then he could drive her into town, drop her off, and never look back.

With a sigh, Brent walked around and opened her door. She sat frozen, eyes fixed on the dark woods around them, still clutching the seat belt stretched across her chest.

"You all right?"

"Yes," she said, her voice rough. "No. I don't know."

Yeah, he could relate. Brent made to rub the back of his neck, then sucked in a sharp breath as a jolt of pain flashed across his knuckles. The sound snapped Kayla out of her momentary paralysis, and she turned to face him as he cradled his hand.

"Oh my gosh, you really did hurt your hand."

"It's nothing."

"No." She scrambled down out of the truck. "No, we need to get you to a doctor."

"I said it's nothing." He turned away. "Besides, we can't go back into town for a few hours. Your biker buddies will be looking for us."

She stepped around him and planted both hands on her hips. "Well, if it's broken, we'll just have to chance it."

"It's not broken," he growled.

"Come on, you big baby. Let me have a look at it."

He stared down at those blue eyes of hers and mentally cursed. Like he had the strength to deny her anything. "Fine."

With great care she took his wrist in her hands and pulled it toward her. Her touch was feather-light on his skin. Gentle, almost a caress. The touch of someone who truly cared.

"What kind of pain are you feeling?"

Brent tried to answer, but his heart was in his throat. He wasn't used to being handled like fine china, to being cared about by anyone but his remaining family. She looked up, concern clear on her face. He swallowed hard and tried again.

"It's not broken, if that's what you're asking."

"How do you know?"

"Because I'm a guy. I know what broken bones feel like because I've broken plenty of them before."

Her right brow arched. "And only guys break bones?"

"Out of stupidity? Yes."

"Okay, I'll agree with you there. But you really should get that checked out."

He slowly extracted his hand from hers. "I think some ice will do the job."

Or some morphine, he thought. Too bad neither could heal the fissure forming in his ironclad heart. *Never should have agreed to meet Miles tonight.*

"Ice would probably be a good thing." She turned back toward the truck, whose passenger door was still hanging wide open. "Just let me grab my...oh."

"Oh, what?"

"My purse. I left it in the booth back at Chevvy's." She put her hands to her cheeks now. "And Tommy—we still need to reach him, let him know I'm okay."

"Here, you can use my phone. I probably still have his number in here from the other day."

Which, of course, he did. Had debated deleting it all weekend, but hadn't been able to bring himself to do so. Because he was a grade A, smitten, pathetic sap.

"No, that won't work. He doesn't have it on him,

accidentally left it at the shop." Kayla dropped her hands to her sides and barked a hopeless laugh. "Brilliant."

"Then I'll just call Miles. He's, uh, there, too."

Brent reached for the cell in his front left pocket, then bit back a curse as his tender knuckles met denim. He blinked away the pain-induced water in his eyes and found Kayla staring up at him, wringing her hands.

"Do you need some help?"

It was an innocent enough question, coming from anyone else. But the woman standing before him wasn't anyone else, nor was she all that innocent. Kayla stepped forward, those unassuming blues locked on his pocket. Slowly she reached out and gave the denim a tug.

"This pocket?"

Brent's mouth went dry. If she touched him again, would he be able to resist touching her as well? Hauling her inside and depositing her on his bed?

The answer to that would be a resounding *no*.

"You know what? Why don't we just go inside? I'll call him from the cordless."

He turned and headed for the back door, grateful to put some distance between them. And while the idea of allowing her in made his palms sweat, the perfect distraction waited inside. One that was sure to keep her occupied. A scratch sounded on the other side of the door.

Key in the lock, he turned back to find Kayla exactly where he'd left her, gaze fixed on the truck and hands wringing once more.

"You coming?"

She looked his way, apprehension clear on her face. "I don't know…"

The pain in his left hand was starting to really hum and what little patience Brent had was diminishing by the second. "I could really use that ice."

Okay, so his answer had come out as nearly a growl. She crossed her arms. And while it would be a whole hell of a lot safer for his libido if she didn't come inside, the gentleman in him wasn't about to leave her out in the elements.

"Besides, you don't want to stand around in the dark for too long," he chided. "Never know when a bear might mosey into the yard."

"A b-bear?"

The sudden panic in her voice brought a grin to his lips. "Yep. There's a black one that tends to hang around here. Guess that's what I get for feeding him."

Kayla hurried to his side, her gaze trained on the woods. "You fed it? What were you thinking?"

A whimper sounded from inside the house, followed by another impatient scratch. Brent coughed over the sound and worked to keep his face neutral.

"Well, he does keep the rabbits away. And I haven't had a rodent problem since he moved in."

She took a step back. "Wait…moved in?"

He turned the key and pushed the door open. In a flash, his six-year-old Newfoundland nosed his way around the door and barreled out. Kayla stumbled back with a shriek as the mass of black fur bore down upon her.

"Kayla," Brent said, "meet Bear. Bear, meet Kayla."

She lost her footing and landed square on her ass. Bear capitalized on the moment and drenched her with licks and kisses.

"No," she cried, bringing her arms up to protect her

head. "Gah, enough already. Enough!"

"Come on now, buddy," Brent said with a chuckle. He laced his good hand through Bear's collar and tugged him off the still-stunned Kayla. "She's not used to having a hundred and fifty pound baby crawling all over her."

Bear whimpered but obeyed. He plopped his butt on the stoop and watched with bright eyes as Kayla slowly rose to her feet. It wasn't often Brent had visitors.

"'A bear hangs around here.'" Kayla swiped a hand across her slobber-coated cheek with narrowed eyes. "Funny, Masterson. Real funny."

He shrugged. "It wasn't a complete lie. Black bears have been known to wander through the area. This one just happens to be of the canine variety."

Bear's tail thumped impatiently against Brent's foot. The stern look on Kayla's face softened.

"Can I pet him?"

"Please, before he spontaneously combusts."

Kayla reached the back of her hand out to Bear. Brent warned his pup to behave, then released his collar. The overgrown fluff ball shuffled forward until his body was pressed up against her legs. Bear offered her hand a kiss. And then another. And then another.

"Hi, Bear," she cooed. "Aren't you just the sweetest thing?"

She bent down, and a broad smile lit her delicate features. Bear craned his neck to lick at her neck and face. Kayla laughed—a pure, unadulterated sound—and continued with her baby talk as she rubbed behind his ears. She looked happy, happier than he'd seen her since their dinner with Ruby and Miles at the inn. Right before she led him upstairs and into her suite. He turned away before the memory of what came next could weave its way into his thoughts and taunt him yet again.

"I really need that ice."

Kayla sat at Brent's dining room table, stroking the top of Bear's head as she scanned the homey décor around her. It was nothing like she would have pictured for its moody, muscle-bound owner, with its cheery rooster-themed wallpaper and worn but spotless Shaker furniture. Then again, maybe this was how the previous owners had decorated it, and he'd never bothered to do any updates. That made more sense. After spending all day working construction, the last thing he probably wanted to do was come home and do more.

Overhead, a board creaked. Brent had come in, filled a plastic bag with ice, set the oven to preheat for a frozen pizza, then mumbled something about needing to change out of his beer-soaked shirt as he walked past. She reminded him to call Miles so he could let Tommy know she was all right, and had gotten nothing more than a grunt in return. Clearly, he was tired of coming to her rescue.

Truth be told, she was tired of needing to be saved.

With a sigh, she closed her eyes and recapped the debacle at Chevvy's. God, she was lucky to have gotten out of there intact. Hopefully Brent was right about his hand not being broken. She felt guilty enough interrupting his weekend time and time again.

"So, why are you still here?"

Kayla opened her eyes to see Brent walk by without a

second glance, his ice-wrapped hand tucked safely into his chest. She sat up straighter, heat flooding her cheeks. Bear, unwilling to lose his personal masseuse, pressed his massive, furry body tighter against her leg. "Excuse me?"

"Here, in Mount Pleasant. I thought you were leaving Saturday," he said as he gingerly slid the pizza into the oven. "As soon as the tow truck pulled you free."

"Oh." Kayla relaxed, but only slightly so. "Trust me, I wanted to get on the road. But when we got there, the driver said my car wasn't drivable. Something about a smashed bumper and sub something or another. So he towed it back to my brother's shop."

"Speaking of which, I called Miles. He said your brother was talking to the cops who showed up after we left, and he promised to let him know you were all right. Thirsty?"

"Yes. Poor Tommy, I bet he was freaking out." *If he even saw any of the fight.* For all she knew, he and Heather had been making out and missed the whole thing.

"Miles will set him straight, and we'll get you back soon enough." Brent pulled two Miller Lites from the refrigerator. "I've got this or water, pick your poison."

"Beer's fine, thanks."

He walked over to the table and set one down, then went to twist the cap off the other and scowled at his iced hand.

"Here, let me help you," Kayla said, reaching for the beer. "It's the least I can do."

"Thanks. So, can Tommy fix your car?"

"He seems to think so," she said, twisting both caps off as he took the seat across from her. "But the parts are going to take a few days to come in."

"That sucks. So, what, you're staying with him in the

meantime?"

"No. His roommate came down with the flu. Tommy's been over at his girlfriend's place."

"So where'd you end up then?" he asked. "Hampton Inn? The Chippewa?"

"Neither. Last night, I stayed at the garage. Tommy keeps a couch up in the loft. I hoped it'd be a one-night deal."

Brent's right brow rose, and heat flooded Kayla's cheeks.

"I mean, you know. Sleeping on the couch. At my brother's. A one-time thing." Lord, she was just digging this hole deeper and deeper.

He stood with a frown and headed back toward the kitchen. When he wasn't laughing and joking, Brent could almost be downright intimidating. Except he wasn't, not to her. Mr. Tough Guy had one giant, soft underbelly. Well, beneath his nicely sculpted six-pack. She lifted the amber bottle to her lips and tried to wash that image from her mind.

"Ruby will be pissed, you know," he said, drawing two plates from his cupboard.

"Because…?"

"Because you traded the Checkerberry Inn for a night on some lumpy couch."

Only Ruby? She pushed the disappointment from her mind—it had no right to be there. "But the inn isn't open for the season. Besides, I wasn't going to make the tow truck driver haul me all the way back out there."

"No," he said, his voice void of humor. "It seems I'm the only one who gets to haul you around town."

The burning in her cheeks intensified. Brent returned with the plates and resumed his place at the table. He took a long drag from his beer, then looked her way. "If I ask you a question, will you give me an honest answer?"

She squirmed beneath the intensity of his gaze. "Maybe."

"You didn't really come up here to visit your brother, did you?"

Kayla tipped her own bottle back and considered her response. She'd danced around the question at dinner on Friday, offered a pseudo-truth about the reason for her trip north. But that had been more about saving face in front of Ruby than anything else. Here, in Brent's kitchen, she felt no need to keep up the charade. Still, his question surprised her.

"Not exactly, no."

"Besides, you were all dressed up for work, which leads me to believe that either (a) you got fired, or (b) something sent you running."

Kayla's eyes narrowed.

"Ah, so you did run away from something."

"I didn't run away. I just…left to get coffee and never went back."

"So you ran away."

Kayla slammed her beer down. "I *didn't* run away."

"What happened at work, Kayla?"

Brent's voice was soft now. Concerned. She looked away.

"Tell me."

Kayla sucked in a deep breath, then slowly released it. She had no idea why he was asking, or why he even seemed to care. Still, she felt an odd compulsion to come clean with him.

"Friday morning I got called into my boss's office and blamed for instigating a malicious prank on our biggest client. Which, of course, I would never, ever do. But instead of believing me when I swore I'd been set up, they handed me a week off with no pay. Technically, it wasn't supposed to start until Monday. I planned to work the rest of the day, but…" She shook her head and sighed.

"Do you know who set you up?"

"Took me until I got up here and told the story to Tommy, but yeah, I figured it out. My boss's worthless stepson. The guy's been trying to outdo me since the day I started there. But he's lazy and doesn't have an eye for design like I do."

Brent scowled. "So, what are you going to do?"

"Go back and find a way to clear my name, try to redeem my reputation. I just haven't figured out how to do that quite yet." She took another sip of her beer, feeling ten pounds lighter now that she'd gotten the "big secret" off her chest. "What would you do if you were me?"

"Me? I'd punch the guy."

They both looked down at his hand, wrapped in ice, and burst out laughing.

Kayla picked at the label on her beer bottle. "Yeah, well, something tells me my punch wouldn't have the same effect."

The oven timer went off, and Brent rose to his feet. "Don't underestimate yourself, Kayla," he said, his face suddenly serious. "Or the power you hold over other people."

With that he walked away, leaving her to wonder what the heck that was all about.

B rent pulled the pizza out a short time later and, as they dug into an incredibly late dinner, he was careful not to bring up anything else about her work. Instead they talked hobbies. They talked baseball and cars. And, trivial as it all was, by the end of their meal he found himself hanging on her every word.

Whether from the beer or the company, Kayla let down her guard. The woman couldn't speak without using her hands to illustrate, and when she talked about the things she enjoyed most, her features took on a youthful glow. She was endearing, adorable, and sharp as a tack. When she smiled, he couldn't help but smile, too. And when she teased him about his favorite ball team—she was a Cards fan, the poor girl—he felt compelled to razz her back. By the end of their meal, Brent felt as though he had an old friend seated across from him, not a near stranger.

Still, he did his best to remember it was all temporary. She wouldn't be here tomorrow, or much longer tonight. Even so, when a knock sounded at his front door midway through their second round of beer, pain still laced itself around his heart.

Kayla threw Brent a quizzical look as Bear started for the door, his tail wagging.

"Expecting someone?" She threw him another one of her teasing grins.

He looked away and reluctantly rose from his chair. "Probably just Miles."

Of course it was Miles, though he couldn't bring himself to tell her. Nor had he been able to admit that his earlier call had involved not only the request from Kayla, but also one of his own. It'd seemed like the right move to make at the time, the safer move, but now he wasn't so sure.

He trudged down the hall, wishing it was someone else—*anyone* else—and yet knowing only Miles's presence had the power to lure Bear from their guest's side. His evening with Kayla had been magical, even more so than their lust-filled fling on Friday. Her musical laughter had breathed life back into his old farmhouse. Hell, had breathed life back into him. When was the last time he'd sat at the kitchen table and shared stories from his youth? Or cooked dinner and ate it somewhere other than in front of the television?

Ah, but that was exactly why she needed to leave. Kayla was a liability—her presence alone jeopardized his very existence. He'd decided long ago to avoid love, to stay single and keep his heart safe. For Brent, love always led to loss, and he didn't possess the strength to survive any more of that.

No, he'd done the right thing, asking Miles to come and take her off his hands. He knew the power she wielded over him and had taken a preemptive step in protecting his heart. So why was he having such a hard time convincing himself to open the door?

"I know you're there, man. Let me in already."

Impatience rang clear in Miles's voice. Asking him to abandon his date after standing him up had been ballsy. But desperate times called for desperate measures. Brent pulled the door open and braced himself for a verbal assault. Surprisingly, the only thing Miles shot his way was a dirty look.

"Thanks for coming, man" Brent said. "Did you talk to her brother?"

"Miles?" Kayla came down the hall and stopped beside Brent. "What are you doing here?"

Miles threw Brent an "are you kidding me?" look, then shook his head and forced a smile onto his lips.

"Well, I wanted to let you know I found your brother. Told him Brent saved your ass. Again."

"Saved all of me, is more like it." Kayla reached out and set her hand on Brent's shoulder. Guilt-induced nausea washed over him, and he bit back the bile creeping up his throat.

"But you didn't have to drive all the way over here to tell me that. Unless…" She grimaced. "Your date didn't go so well tonight, did it?"

Miles's eyes narrowed as his gaze settled on Brent. "Not the way I'd planned it would, no."

"Aw, I'm so sorry to hear that."

"He'll get over it," Brent said, a warning in his tone.

Kayla nodded, unaware of the brewing tension. "So, did Tommy and Heather stick around to eat after you talked to them?"

"Yeah. But it was more sucking the sauce off each other's fingers than anything else."

Kayla's face twisted in disgust. "Thanks, Miles—I'm gonna have that image burned into my mind all night."

"You and me both," he said with a wink. "So that reminds me, your purse is in the car. You want a ride back into town?"

"A ride? Thanks, but I think Brent was planning to take me back later."

Miles's gaze shifted to his. Brent hated himself for what he was about to do, but it had to be done. He leveled a stern look at Kayla.

"I think you should go. With Miles."

Guilt riddled Brent as a medley of emotions washed across her face. Confusion, understanding, rejection. She looked down at her hands for a moment. When she looked back up, Kayla wore a cool, careful facade.

"Fine. Just let me get my wallet."

She strode into the kitchen long enough to grab her wallet, then returned to the front room and stepped around him to pat Bear farewell. The giant ball of fur leaned into her and whimpered, sensing she was about to leave. Leave, and never come back.

"Thank you, Brent," she said, darting a quick look and polite smile in his direction as she made her way for the door. "For dinner, and another rescue. I'm sure it'll be a relief not to have to save me again."

"Kayla, it's not—" He shook his head. It was no use trying to talk his way out of this. The best he could do now was let her go and try his best to forget her.

Miles watched Kayla brush past him, then turned a wary eye on Brent. For once, the first thing out of his mouth wasn't a smart-ass comment. "You gonna be all right, man?"

Brent wanted to say yes, to put on a brave face and tell his cousin he was right as rain. But the pain of knowing how much she must hate him right now rendered him silent. Miles studied him a moment more, then clapped a gentle hand on Brent's shoulder. "Call me if you need anything."

Miles stepped outside, and Brent resisted the urge to follow. Instead, he closed the door and headed for the kitchen to clean up. To wipe away any evidence that Kayla had ever been there. As he did so, he told himself over and over he'd done the right thing.

Because if she'd stayed another hour, it would have turned into two. And if she'd stayed for two, it would have turned into the entire night. His willpower would have eventually crumbled, and he would have carried her up to his bed and made love to her. And in the morning he would have awakened to find her body perfectly entwined with his again.

That image, above all else, had scared him into asking for Miles's help. It would have killed Brent to wake with her at his side once more. Because if there ever was a next time, Brent wasn't sure he'd have the strength to let her go.

Chapter Eleven

Kayla climbed into the front passenger seat of Miles's cherry red Camaro, trying her best to keep it together. She wanted to hit something. Or cry. Or maybe do a little of both. All she knew was the sooner she could get away from Brent, the better.

She snapped her seat belt into place and cast a scowl out into the dark woods. What was with that man? One minute he played hero, the next he's handing her off like yesterday's dirty laundry. Had she done something wrong? Said something inappropriate? No, she couldn't think of anything. Maybe the guy just had issues.

Or maybe Kayla needed to stop letting her guard down. Wasn't that the real reason she'd fallen prey to that stupid stunt at work? She'd started to soften up, interact on a more personal level with her ad team, and look what that had cost her.

The driver's side door opened, and Miles slid into his

seat. "Where to, Little Miss Indiana?"

"Back to town, I guess. My brother's shop is across from that hardware store on East Broadway." She threw him an apologetic look. "Sorry you got roped into playing taxi driver tonight."

"'S all right," he said with a shrug. "Date wasn't going so well, anyway."

"They never do, when you have to cut them short to go run favors."

"Not so much, no."

He offered her a teasing grin as he turned his key in the ignition. Still, she felt badly for ruining his night. Come to think of it, all she'd done was ruin peoples' nights tonight. Hers included.

"So, what's with him, anyway?" she asked once they were back out on the main road.

"Brent?" Miles glanced up at his rearview mirror, as if checking to ensure his cousin wasn't within earshot. "He's just a bit complicated, that's all."

"Complicated? Is that what you call it? I would have guessed bipolar."

"Aw, now, don't let his mood swings get to you. He's been through a lot. More than anyone should ever have to."

Kayla stared out the windshield. She shouldn't care about what he'd been through. Shouldn't want to know any more at all about the big jerk. And yet, she did. "Oh?"

"It might be hard to imagine, but Brent used to be a pretty easygoing guy. Well-loved, adventurous, funny. Growing up, the girls couldn't get enough of him."

She could easily picture it. When Brent smiled—which he'd actually done quite a bit tonight before he'd kicked her out—his usual, standoffish facade was replaced with something entirely more…inviting. And, as she'd witnessed first-hand in her suite Friday night, he definitely had the total package to back up that invitation.

"So what happened? He get cut from the varsity football squad or something?"

"Oh, hell no," Miles said. "Coach Smith would have walked across hot coals before doing that. Brent was one badass tight end, among other things. But that was before the crash."

"Crash? He was in some kind of accident?"

"No, not Brent. His parents. They were on a plane, coming back for our college graduation. Their flight was due to touch down a few hours before the ceremony." Miles grew quiet for a moment, then shook his head. "I was there when he got the call. To say he was devastated would be an understatement."

"Oh, how awful."

A shocked numbness washed over Kayla. Losing her mother to cancer had been bad enough. But to lose both parents at the same time without warning? She couldn't even begin to imagine what that would have done to her.

"Brent loved his parents; he was always really close with both of them. When they died, a piece of him died, too.

"At the time," Miles continued after a moment, "all I could think was thank God he still had Nikki."

"Is that his sister?"

"No, Brent's an only child. Nikki was his girlfriend. She was the glue that held him together when he went through his own personal hell. Without her there, I don't know how he would have survived it all."

Kayla could see the parallels between Brent's nightmare and her own. Tommy had been her Nikki, her rock. But her brother had relied on Kayla as well, and together they'd walked away from their mother's death stronger. Closer. She wished the same had been true of her father.

"So, how long has it been?" she asked. "Since his parents died?"

"We graduated from Central Michigan the summer of 2006, so almost eight years now."

Eight years. Kayla's own mother had been gone a little over six. She'd hoped the pain would eventually diminish, the loneliness subside. Not a day went by when she wasn't haunted by the loss. But if Brent had become a shell of his former self even with the help of a steady girlfriend, Kayla couldn't help but wonder if her future was destined to remain bleak. She hadn't had a significant other there to comfort and carry her.

Then again, where was Nikki now? Kayla hadn't seen any pictures of a woman at Brent's house. And there was the whole Friday night fling they'd had. Definitely no ring on the man's finger...

"Yep, eight years ago," Miles said, his tone taking on a harder edge. "And Nikki left him six months later."

"Wait, *what*?" Kayla turned in her seat to face him. "How could she leave him in the middle of all that?"

"Because she's a selfish, two-timing wench, that's why." Miles's gaze flashed momentarily to hers. "Sorry, but I have a hard time speaking kindly about the woman."

"Sounds to me like she earned that designation all on her own."

The growl in her response surprised Kayla, as did the

anger bubbling inside her. She held no claim to Brent, and yet she found herself wanting to pummel this Nikki chick. Soundly.

"Yes, she did." Miles grinned. "I like you, Indiana."

"Thanks," she said, then mumbled, "At least someone around here does."

"Oh, you've got more than one fan in Mount Pleasant. Trust me."

"True, I've always got Tommy."

"That's not who I was talking about," Miles said, his voice softer now.

"Ruby, then?"

"Try again."

Kayla studied his profile. No grin. Who was even left?

"Surely you're not talking about your cousin. The one who summoned you away from your date to play taxi driver?"

"Look, if there's anyone who knows Brent, it's me. And ever since you showed up this weekend, he's been...different. Like the old Brent is still in there somewhere, trying to break free."

"Pfft, right. Maybe he just woke up Friday and decided to turn over a new leaf," she said, ignoring the dirty look Miles shot her. "Or maybe he's looking forward to working for Ruby now. You never know, some hot little number could book a room at the inn and take his breath away."

Miles wove through the quiet streets and pulled to a halt before Tommy's shop. Then he turned and studied her for a moment. "Maybe she already did."

"Huh?"

Miles's right brow lifted.

"He told you, didn't he."

"Didn't have to," Miles said, a smooth grin stretching across his face. "I found him hiding in the barn yesterday morning, sipping coffee and watching the sunrise. Haven't seen him look that relaxed in years."

Kayla felt fire consume her cheeks. "Look, Miles, I'm not usually the type—"

"I don't judge, so save your breath." His gaze shifted from hers to the old, run-down storefront before them. "You aren't really sleeping here tonight, are you?"

She tipped her chin up. "As a matter of fact, I am. Not that it's any of your business."

"No, of course not," he said, then looked down at his cuticles. "Nice and cheap."

"Exactly."

Miles nodded. "Any mice?"

"Just one."

She reached for the door. He was up to something, and Kayla wasn't in the mood to play games. In fact, after the evening's drama, a quiet night with Mickey was starting to sound good.

"It's too bad, really," he said.

Don't do it, she told herself. *Don't ask and don't encourage.* She needed her space, needed to get away from the drama. But as her gaze flashed to the shop's second-story window, the kink in her back reminded her she could also really use a decent bed to crash on.

Darn it.

"What?" she asked through clenched teeth. "What's too bad?"

"Oh, you know, that you're stuck sleeping here when there's a whole inn full of nice, comfy beds back at the

Checkerberry."

"Yeah? Well last I heard, it wasn't open for the season yet. And even if it was, I couldn't afford to stay there all week. I have car repairs to pay for, remember?"

"Ah, but that's just it. You need a place to stay, and Ruby needs help getting the place ready to open."

"What are you talking about? She's got two strapping grandsons, what else could she need?"

"An extra set of hands," he said. "Our landscaping hasn't been touched yet this spring. Ruby's just getting too old to be mending flower beds and hauling mulch. And Brent's up to his eyeballs in renovations."

"What about you?" she asked. "What's wrong with your hands?"

"Nope, I'm swamped with my own work. Besides, I do numbers, not landscaping."

"So hire someone. A college kid or something."

Miles shook his head. "You're not following me, Indiana. See, you need a place to stay—no, don't argue, just listen—and I need some free manual labor. It's a win-win for everyone involved."

"No."

"Come on. You know how to use a shovel, right?"

"Of course I know how to use a shovel," she snapped. "I just…haven't for a few years."

Kayla looked away. Shovels made her think of flowers, and flowers made her think of her mother. That dull ache in her chest returned.

"Well, here's your chance to get back into practice."

She shook her head. "I…can't, Miles. I just can't."

"Suit yourself."

Kayla pushed the door open and stepped out onto the curb. A moment ago, a quiet night to herself sounded heavenly. Now, as she looked out at the cold, silent shop, she dreaded it. The passenger window rolled down behind her.

"Last chance. This place and a week of boredom, or the Checkerberry and your fill of fresh air, sunshine, and Ruby's cooking."

She hesitated. Looked back and met Miles's gaze.

Lord, his offer was tempting. A comfortable room of her own. Warm showers. Hot breakfasts. Surely she could control her emotions while she worked on the landscaping. It wasn't like she was back at her parents' place, having to face the daffodils. Ah, but there was someone at the inn she'd have to face. Someone who'd made it clear tonight that he wanted nothing more to do with her.

"What about Brent?"

"You don't have to say one word to Mr. Unsociable," Miles said. "My guess is he'll steer clear of you during your stay anyway."

Still... "But I brought work with me."

It wasn't a complete lie, since she did plan on finding a way to smooth over all of this with her boss. Then again, how was she going to do all that without a decent internet connection? Did this town have a Starbucks with wifi? If so, she could always camp out there...

"Aw, who wants to do work when you're on vacation?"

"Says the guy who's asking me to come and work at his grandmother's inn while I'm on this so-called vacation."

Miles's lips drew into a pout. "Please don't make me beg, Kayla. You need a place to stay, we need help getting the inn ready for opening. There's no time clock, no set schedule.

You do what you can to help, and we make sure you have a warm bed to fall into each night."

"God, I'm an idiot for doing this." Kayla yanked the car door open and slid back inside. "Fine, I'll do it. For Ruby."

"Atta girl."

"Just don't go getting any crazy ideas about trying to set me up with your cousin."

Miles shot her an innocent look. "I wouldn't dream of it."

"Good," Kayla said, crossing her arms over her chest. "Because once my car's done, I am outta here."

Miles shifted into drive, and the farther they drove from the shop, the more Kayla's confidence in her decision dimmed. She'd done the right thing, hadn't she? What could she possibly stand to lose in this unexpected arrangement? There was no money involved, no script to be followed. And yet, she couldn't help but be wary. Because while her stay at the Checkerberry might seem to be free of charge, there was no guarantee it wouldn't ultimately cost her something much more valuable.

Her heart.

Chapter Twelve

Monday morning dawned bright and sunny, not a cloud in the sky. The weekend's wintery mix had been replaced by an unusually warm and dry forecast. Gone was the musty, damp chill in the air, and yesterday's sunshine seemed to have dried the Checkerberry's grounds considerably.

Too bad the weather was doing nothing to clear Kayla from his mind. Only a day of backbreaking labor might be able to do that. Even then, Brent's chances were still slim to none.

I never should have gone to that stupid bar last night, he thought for the hundredth time as he drove his truck to the far corner of Ruby's property. Never should have played the Good Samaritan on Friday, either. Sure, he'd finally gotten laid, but was a night of passion really worth all this heartache?

Miles would say hell yes. Though that was because the man seemed to have no conscience when it came to loving and leaving the beauties of Mount Pleasant. Brent, however, wasn't wired like that. Sometimes, he wished he was.

Like now.

He parked the Silverado near a damaged section of fence that separated Ruby's land from that of her neighbor, Hank Billings. It'd been Hank's wife's brilliant idea a few years back to start raising alpacas. They're beautiful, she'd said. Their fleece will bring us money, he'd said.

They've gone and broken my darned fence again, is what Ruby said. Again, and again, and again.

"Mindless beasts," Brent grumbled, surveying the most recent damage.

Actually, it wasn't so much that they were mindless as they seemed to be running around blind—with desire. Either the Billings were feeding them aphrodisiacs, or it was mating season. Brent shook his head, trying to free his mind from the scene he'd discovered behind the barn just this morning. All that braying and grunting. Christ, he'd about lost his breakfast.

The worst part was, four-legged fence-wreckers or not, at least they had mates. All he had was his work and a hairy black beast named Bear. Which was all he really needed, he reminded himself as he dragged the broken railing aside. And the sooner he got that through his thick skull, the better.

Brent pulled on a pair of work gloves and set about wrestling the fence post loose from its hole in the ground. The sun beat down on his back, and in no time he'd broken a sweat. Soon he stopped to strip out of his fleece outer layer. A blue jay cried in the distance, drawing Brent's gaze out over the hilly green countryside. The sight was as familiar to him as breathing; he'd been over every inch of Ruby's land more times than he could count. And yet, the joy that sight usually brought evaded him this morning.

It was no great mystery why. And though he'd ordered himself to push her from his thoughts, the memory of Kayla continued to haunt him. Their time together last night had been like a shot of endorphins straight to his heart, jump-starting the organ from its long-dormant state. As much as he'd tried not to start falling for her, somehow he still had.

Which was why sending her off before things went any further last night had been the right call to make. He knew the agony he felt after her departure would eventually subside. In the meantime, it served as the perfect reminder to his earlier conclusion: Kayla was dangerous. Her mere presence was a crowbar aimed at the lock around his heart.

A lock he couldn't afford to lose.

Brent spent the rest of the morning mending damaged sections of Ruby's fence. At one point she and Miles passed by in the distance during her weekly scan of the grounds. They neither drove the inn's Gator yard cart his way to stop and visit nor bothered with a wave, which was fine with Brent. He was too busy wrestling his own demons to want company. Though it did amuse him to see Miles dressed down for once, wearing some old CMU shirt and a Yankees cap. Whether from the lure of sunshine or Ruby's taunting, his cousin had finally given in and agreed to help with the landscaping.

About damned time, with their opening less than two weeks off.

When Brent made it back up to the inn and headed around to the front porch for an afternoon of scraping and priming, he couldn't help but give his cousin some grief when he spotted that navy cap hovering above Ruby's nearby spring blooms.

"Well, well, well," he said, dropping his supplies near

the front steps. "It seems you aren't allergic to manual labor after all."

The Yankees cap dipped and shook. When its brim rose again, the last face he expected to see at the Checkerberry came into view. One that had haunted him all day, just as it'd haunted his dreams the past few nights.

Kayla.

Anger welled up inside of him. Anger toward his meddling cousin. Anger toward his meddling grandmother. And anger at himself, for the way his heart rate spiked at the sight of her.

"What are you doing here?" Brent demanded, eyes dark as Friday's storm.

Kayla sat back on her heels and reminded herself that she was here for Ruby. Ruby needed help, and Kayla needed a place to lay her weary head. And, after the day she'd had, the Jacuzzi tub in her suite was sounding mighty good right about now. No way was she going to let Brent intimidate her into leaving. He didn't own the place, Ruby did. And Ruby had been ecstatic when she learned Kayla was back.

The two women had spent the entire morning together. Ruby took her on a grand tour of the property, showcasing the barn, the pond and its pier, and the trails through the woods. At one point they'd spotted Brent wrestling with a fence post well off the cleared trail. Relief had washed over her when Ruby had kept on driving—she'd been worried since agreeing to this arrangement how their next meeting would go. So far, it had gone as expected. Question was, could she keep her cool?

"Well, hello, Brent. Nice to see you again, too."

He remained on the porch, fuming but silent.

"Have any luck with that fence? Ruby told me about how those llama-things are always knocking them down."

"Alpacas," he said, his voice low and deadly. "And yes, the fence is fixed. Now answer the question."

Kayla rose from the flower bed and put a hand to her back. Working Ruby's landscaping was no different than what she did every year for her father's yard. And yet, somehow she always forgot to stop and stretch often enough. Yep, the Jacuzzi tub was definitely in her future tonight.

"What I'm doing here?" A small part of her rather enjoyed seeing him like this, all out of sorts. She tugged off the gloves Ruby had loaned her and motioned toward the nearest flower bed. "Well, isn't it obvious?"

Brent growled, turned, and dismounted the porch. In a flash he was toe-to-toe with her, his hands like vise grips on her upper arms. "Why? Why did you come back?"

"Hey! Let me go!"

His gaze fixed on hers, unmoved. "No. Not until you tell me what's going on."

"Miles said—"

"I *knew* it."

His hands released her then, and Kayla stumbled to regain her balance. She watched as he turned back toward the front door.

"Oh no you don't." She tossed her gloves down and ran ahead of him, blocking his path. "You leave Miles alone."

Brent's brows rose in unison on his smooth forehead. "Oh, Miles has a new member of his fan club, does he? Tell me, did you take him back to your room, too?"

Kayla's hand moved of its own accord, and pain flared across her palm as it connected with his cheek. Brent flinched but otherwise remained motionless. Almost instantly, a red handprint appeared upon the point of impact.

"I suppose I deserved that," he said after a moment, his voice low, strained.

"What I do and who I do it with is none of your business. And for the record? Miles offered me a place to stay in exchange for helping Ruby get ready for the season opening. Because everyone here is already swamped.

"Besides, I already learned my lesson about allowing Masterson boys into my room." She stormed back across the yard to retrieve her gloves, hand trowel, and shovel. "And it won't happen again."

He said nothing as she rounded the far corner of the building, nor did he make any move to stop her. The farther she got from the man, the angrier she became. How dare he insinuate she'd slept with Miles. Or demand to know why she was here. Who the hell did he think he was?

Kayla discarded her tools in the small shed that doubled as the Checkerberry's pool house with a scowl, then headed inside. No way was she going to work out there while Brent was around. She stopped at the inn's back door and kicked off her shoes. It was then that she caught sight of her reflection. Kayla had forgotten all about the CMU shirt Miles had loaned her. And the borrowed Yankees cap. Is that where he'd gotten that asinine idea that she'd slept with his cousin? Just because she was wearing a few articles of his clothing?

What difference did it make to him, anyway? He'd sent her off the night before, probably couldn't get rid of her fast enough, and now he was acting like he owned her?

"Is that you, Kayla?"

So much for heading upstairs to punch a few pillows. "Yeah, be right there."

She headed in the direction of Miles's voice and found him in an office toward the end of the next hallway. The room was small and cozy but cramped with a large, L-shaped desk eating up a good half of the space. On the far wall stood a matching bookshelf, filled to the brim with thick textbooks on a topic that would put her right to sleep: accounting. Her gaze shifted to the man behind the desk.

"What's up?"

Miles pushed back from his computer and smiled. "So? How'd it go?"

"Really well, until your cousin showed up. So much for me not having to talk to him." Kayla tugged the ball cap off with a frown and tossed it to him.

Miles grimaced and set the cap aside. "Shit, I'm sorry. He's just—"

"Been through a lot. I get it. But still." She blew out a frustrated sigh. "Anyway, I got further than I thought I would today. You can go ahead and order that mulch for tomorrow. I should be ready for it by midday. I'm guessing there's a wheelbarrow around here somewhere I can borrow?"

"Oh, I can do better than that. We've got a Gator."

"A what?"

"A Gator. You know, like a golf cart on steroids. Has a dump bed and everything."

"Sweet."

She looked out the window and couldn't help but wonder what kind of damage this Gator might do to a grumpy groundskeeper? The good girl in her *tsk-tsked* the idea. The bad girl side? She cheered. Too bad she'd never actually do it. Besides, the big lug would probably put one heck of a dent in Ruby's cart. With a sigh, Kayla shifted her gaze back inside.

"So, this is your office, huh? Nice."

"Thanks. My grandfather made all the furniture by hand. Most of it from wood right here on the property." He gave the desk a loving pat; the motion drew Kayla's eye to a sketch near his hand.

"Whatcha working on?"

"Oh this? Just some doodles of an ad idea I've been chewing on."

She pulled the paper closer and slipped without thought into work mode. An ad like this would never fly at Wayne. Not because his artwork was awful—and it was, she'd seen third graders do better—but because the design was all wrong. Years of practice, though, kept her from saying as much. Instead, she did what she loved to do: offered feedback and steered him in a new and improved direction.

"Not bad. Though it might grab your audience's attention faster if you made the tag line smaller and moved it there, shortened this sentence here, and then maybe added a picture of the front of the inn behind it all." She looked up to find him staring at her with mouth ajar and shrugged. "Just a thought."

He blinked a few times and pulled the sketch back to his side of the desk. "Well, great. I'll, uh, take that under consideration."

She rose to her feet and put a hand to the aching spot in her lower back. "Well, if you'll excuse me, the Jacuzzi tub's calling my name."

"Enjoy," Miles mumbled, still staring at the sketch she'd just critiqued.

Kayla left his office and headed upstairs to her suite. Once there, she locked the door behind her and went straight for the Jacuzzi tub. It was either that or go back downstairs to strangle Brent Masterson, and she simply didn't have the energy to do that. As it was, she barely had enough energy to strip out of her filthy clothes.

Soon she slipped gingerly into a tub full of steaming water and rested her head on its back ledge. As the jets worked their magic on her aching body, Kayla began to wonder how she'd ever be able to keep her end of the bargain with Miles if Brent was going to accost her every day. Soft bed or not, she wasn't going to hang around and be bullied—she already suffered through enough of that at work. Too bad she couldn't stay inside the rest of the week and develop bold new ads for the inn instead.

Develop bold new ads.

A grin tugged at Kayla's lips. The upcoming Follinger bid. If she could coach her team offsite to win that major project, Jacober would have no choice but to bring her back. And if she built the profit margin just right, maybe he'd even pay her for the week. But to do all that, she'd need the inn's internet connection, at least until her car was fixed and ready to go.

Now that would make enduring the grouch a bit more bearable.

Chapter Thirteen

Brent remained on the porch long after his altercation with Kayla, scraping and sanding away his frustrations. His cheek still stung from Kayla's slap, but not as much as his ego. He'd been completely out of line with that comment about her sleeping with Miles, he knew that. She'd said she wasn't usually a one-night stand kind of girl, and he believed her. Didn't make having to endure the sight of her for the duration of her stay any easier. Then again, he wouldn't have seen her or acted like a total jerk if Miles hadn't brought her back to the inn.

What was his cousin playing at?

Oh sure, Kayla could insist all day long that Miles's intentions were harmless or selfless. But Brent knew his cousin better. Miles never acted without reason. Usually, the reason was centered around self gain. But what could he possibly gain from convincing Kayla to stay at the inn? Was she his next romantic target?

Not likely. While Miles loved to consider himself a ladies' man, he was much more prone to being one-and-done when it came to dates with out-of-towners. To bring her here for an extended stay just didn't fit Miles's M.O.

So, why bring Kayla back at all?

The front door creaked open behind him, then banged shut. A quick glance back found Miles approaching. It took everything Brent had not to leave his post on the stepladder and greet his cousin with a solid right hook. But that would only add fuel to Kayla's fiery temper, something he didn't want to do. One slap a decade was more than enough.

"You calling it a day?"

"Yeah," Miles said. "If I stare at that screen much longer, I'll go cross-eyed."

"You've been at it a lot here lately. In there planning world domination or what?"

"I always put in a lot of time at the office," Miles said. "You're just not usually around to notice."

"I notice more than you think."

Miles frowned. "Meaning?"

Brent studied his cousin for a moment before answering. Miles's face gave away nothing. No mischief, no ulterior motives. And yet, Brent sensed he was definitely up to something.

"Why'd you bring her back here, Miles?"

"Kayla? I thought you were behind schedule."

"Of course I'm behind," Brent said, climbing down off the ladder. "I've been behind all spring. How is her being here supposed to make things any better? She's corporate America, man. Not exactly the caliber worker I need help from right now."

"She said she had some experience with landscaping." Miles looked out over the front yard. "And from the looks of things, I'd say I have to believe her."

Brent's gaze followed his cousin's. He'd been too pissed off earlier to bother inspecting the work she'd done. Now he scanned a critical eye across the yard…and was stunned by the view.

The flower beds bordering the front drive had been cleared of last year's old growth and neatly edged. So had the beds along the front walk and half the length of the porch. Shrubs had been pruned and clematis restrung to the lamppost along the front drive. If Brent didn't know better, he would have guessed a professional landscape crew had spent a day in the yard.

"She asked to have mulch delivered tomorrow," Miles continued. "So don't take the Gator out—I said she could use it. Though, after whatever you said to her earlier, you might want to steer clear of her while she's behind the wheel."

Brent shook his head, still in awe of the view. "I need to give the princess more credit."

"Maybe you need to give us all more credit." Miles gestured toward Brent's cheek. "You hurt yourself today?"

"Uh, yeah. Wasn't paying attention to what I was doing," he said, rubbing a hand absently over the spot where Kayla had slapped him. "It's nothing."

"Well, try to be more careful, will ya? I didn't bring in extra help so you could ease up any." Miles threw him a grin, then turned to leave. But Brent's curiosity wasn't quite sated.

"What did Ruby say about that offer you were telling me about this weekend?"

"Nothing, I haven't mentioned it to her yet. Been going

back and forth between our attorneys, trying to work out the best deal possible." His cousin lowered his voice and cast a wary look toward the front door. "Was waiting until then to bring it up."

"Or waiting for a time when I wouldn't be around." *Or be too distracted.*

Miles's eyes narrowed. "I don't care if you're there or not. It's her inn, her future. Her decision."

"That's right." Brent walked over to where his cousin stood. "*Her* decision, not ours."

"Which I've always respected, so don't make me out to be a wolf in sheep's clothing, Brent. Look, we're all doing our damnedest to keep this place from going belly-up, but it's not enough. The economy, the age of this place… the odds just aren't in our favor. If a solid offer comes along, she'd be a fool not to take it."

"There's got to be something we're missing, something that could help get the inn back on the map."

"Now that you mention it…"

Brent cast him a wary look. "What?"

Miles dug a piece of paper out of his pocket, unfolded it, and showed it to him. "You see this?"

"Cute. Some guest's kid leave that behind?"

"No, smart-ass, I drew that. It's an ad I was toying with, in case this offer falls through."

"So?"

"So your little girlfriend just dissected it without even trying. Gave me pointers I plan to run with and hope to turn into gold."

"She's not my girlfriend," Brent said with a frown.

"Oh, that's right—you've sworn off dating. Well, news

flash, big guy: she's into you. And if you're really looking for a way to save the inn? She's upstairs in her suite, washing you right out of her hair."

Brent grimaced as the image of Kayla's face, full of rage and defiance, came to mind—now was definitely not the time to go asking for help. "I don't think she's as into me as you think."

"And I think you're blind. You asked why I brought her back? I brought her back for you. Because she's the first girl I've seen affect you in years. And you seem to have the same effect on her, too."

"Affect me? Only because I keep running into her."

"Whatever. Look, even if you plan to push her away like all the others, think about this: Kayla could be the exact thing we've been looking for, the spark that could bring the inn back to life. So don't just walk away in a huff like usual. Think about how her advertising prowess could help Ruby, help all of us."

Brent stared at Miles as the truth of his words sank in. He was right—Kayla was the first woman to get past his usual line of defenses in a long, long time. Since Nikki. That's why he'd been trying so hard to push her away, to keep his distance. But what if Miles was right? What if she could help save the inn? Save Ruby's hopes and dreams? Hell, save his own? Who was he to ignore the virtual gift bestowed upon them?

All it would cost him was his heart.

He let out a long sigh. "Wow, coz. Nothing like setting the weight of the world on my shoulders."

"Anytime, man. Anytime. Now, if you'll excuse me, I have a date to get ready for. And you..." He reached out and patted Brent's arm. "Have some thinking to do."

"Lucky me."

His gaze shifted back to the second floor. Too bad he wasn't lucky. Not one bit.

Kayla sat across from her brother at a nearby Dairy Queen an hour later, each with a red plastic spoon and large Blizzard before them. His offer to rescue her from the inn for a few hours had instantly lifted her spirits, and she'd never been one to turn down ice cream. Ever.

"So how's your roommate feeling?"

"I stopped over earlier to check on him, and he still looks green. Whatever Jeremy caught, it's one nasty bug. I'm starting to wonder if we'll need to condemn the place after this."

Kayla laughed. "I don't know who I feel worse for: Jeremy, or the bathroom."

"Right? And I've been stuck at Heather's because Rex walked into the shop this morning and found everything covered with flying ants. Had to call the exterminator; they bombed the place."

"Wow, and I thought my luck was bad." Kayla chuckled. "So, how are things with you and Heather?"

Tommy shrugged. "Can't complain."

Kayla grinned. Tommy had never been one to kiss and tell. Then again, she was his sister, after all. He changed the subject.

"So, any word from the board?"

"No, but it's still early. I'm not even sure when they'll

meet to review my little boo-boo."

"You really want to go back and work there, after this BS suspension?"

"Do I have a choice? I've got bills to pay, Tommy. And I love my job. Well, I did, anyway."

"I say you tell them to shove it and go find a new one. At a place that actually respects you."

Kayla laughed. "Me, just up and quit at Wayne? Yeah, that'd go over well with Dad."

She'd been so excited when her father's old college roomie granted her an interview at Wayne Advertising right after graduation. Thrilled to discover Jacober was not only the hiring manager, but also the head of the company. It seemed like a brilliant stroke of luck. But over time the connection between the two men had become shackles around her wrists. To leave Wayne would be a serious letdown to her father, not to mention a major source of worry she refused to inflict on him. And without another job already lined up, she couldn't afford to walk away even if she wanted to.

Besides, Kayla Daniels was no quitter.

She stabbed at her Blizzard then froze. Isn't that exactly what she'd done this afternoon after Brent yelled at her? And Friday, back at work? What was wrong with her lately?

"Speaking of Dad," Tommy said, "when was the last time you called him?"

"Yesterday morning," she said, preoccupied. "Why?"

"Well, he called earlier to say hi, then asked if he could talk to you for a minute."

"Oh crap. What did you say?"

"I lied and said you and Heather had gone shopping, and that you'd call him when you got back. But I don't think he was buying it."

"Great. So now what do I tell him?"

"How about the truth?"

"No. I refuse to stress him out with all of this."

"Kay, it's *Dad*. You don't have to handle him with kid gloves, for crying out loud. It's not like he's made of glass."

"Neither was mom, but we both know how that ended."

The words slipped out before she realized it and hung in the air between them. Tommy dropped his spoon into the cup before him and sighed. "Is that what this is about? You're worried that stress might—"

"Yes, I am. And it's my job to see that it doesn't."

Tommy frowned. "You can't hover over him or try to shield him from stress or bad news forever. Those things are a part of life."

"Yeah, well, I think he's gone through enough bad news for one lifetime. And shielding him from this little fiasco of mine can't hurt anything. I'll find a way to make things right at work, and he'll be none the wiser."

"But he'd want to know, to comfort you or help you find a way to make it right. That's what dads do."

Truth rang clear in his words. Growing up, their father had been a loving, supportive man. After their mother had been diagnosed with cancer, though, the sparkle in his eyes began to fade. When she passed away, the jovial, exuberant side of their father went to the grave with her. It'd taken years for him to climb out of there, longer than either of his kids. Kayla hated the idea of any setbacks.

"Maybe you're right," she said.

"Of course I'm right. Just call him, okay? Tell him what's going on. Who knows what he'll do if you don't?"

Kayla shot him a grin, then dug out another scoop of Blizzard. What would her father say if she told him about her suspension when she called later? He'd probably insist she march back into work and demand to be reinstated. Which she would, once the Follinger bid's design work was completed. If it turned out half as good as she planned, they'd have to pay her for the week. Or promote her.

Only one way to find out—she needed to get back to the inn and start drafting ideas on how best to rally her team. Kayla didn't need her dad to pull strings, she just had to stop sulking, pull up her big girl panties, and focus. No more letting the Checkerberry's sullen, grouchy handyman distract her, no matter how desirable he may be.

"Fine. But right now, I have bigger things to worry about."

"Oh yeah? Like what?"

She threw her brother a sly grin. "Like how I'm going to convince your girlfriend to let me borrow some clothes that might get a bit dirty the next few days."

Chapter Fourteen

Brent stood on the third rung of his stepladder, his gaze revolving between a can of primer and the woman at the far corner of the building doing her damnedest to ignore him. Yesterday, he'd have been fine with that. More than fine. But that was before he learned she might be able to help save the inn.

He dipped his brush into the primer, then dragged it along the porch wall just below the ceiling, wishing for the dozenth time he hadn't been such an ass to her yesterday. Sure, he'd been beyond frustrated to find her here, but she wasn't to blame. Nor was Miles, though Brent would never say that out loud. No, the outburst was all on him, his anger boiled over from allowing himself to grow too fond of her, to get so close to letting her in.

Now she probably hated him for it.

Which, at the time, had been the response he'd been looking for. It was safer for him if she was mad, safer if she pushed him away. But safer wouldn't keep the inn open, and taking care of his grandmother took precedence over protecting his heart.

Damn it.

He dipped his brush back into the primer and sighed. Why him? Why couldn't she have collided with Miles? Been into the guy who loved women being into him?

It had been a surprising boost to his ego when she'd chosen him over his playboy cousin, though. Brent cast another glance in her direction, and caught a sneak peek of cleavage as she bent forward to retrieve her trowel. As she walked around the corner and out of sight, his mind went right back to their night together, the way she'd—

"Will you be joining us for lunch today, dear?"

"Son of a—" He teetered on the ladder in surprise. Only by some small miracle did he manage not to fall or drop his paint supplies. Once he was sure the hammering in his chest wasn't the precursor to a full-out heart attack, he turned his gaze upon his stealthy grandmother. "Sorry, Ruby. I didn't hear you coming."

"I'm not surprised, what with your heart pounding so loudly for Miss Daniels."

"My heart is pounding because you scared the bejeezus out of me."

"Hmm, perhaps." She looked up at him, too wise for her own good. "Though after the way you've been straining all morning to catch another peek at her from up there, I would have guessed differently."

Busted. Not good, since his grandmother had always been a hopeless romantic. Brent did his best to act indifferent on the subject as he drew his angled brush along the top of the porch wall. "And I thought you always said you'd never turn into one of those old biddies who like to peek out windows and watch people all day long."

Ruby answered with an unladylike snort. "I've hardly stooped to any such level. Now, if you're done insulting your elders, will you kindly answer my original question?"

"Your original question…" Brent lowered his brush, dipped it into the small tray of paint atop his ladder, and tried like mad to think of what that question even was. As usual, once Kayla came up in conversation, his thoughts scattered. It was incredibly frustrating, to say the least.

"Yes, yes, about lunch, dear. Will you be joining us or not?"

"Oh." Brent cast another glance in Kayla's direction. Lunch would be a good time to break the ice. Test the waters and see if there was any hope of an amicable reconciliation between them. If he could just get her to smile again, earn even the tiniest bit of her trust back, maybe that would lead to more. Then again, if she was furious with him and he went and said the wrong thing… "Uh, no. Thank you, but I really need to knock out as much as I can while the weather holds. Chance of rain in the forecast later this week."

"Hmmpf. Chance of your heart shriveling up from inactivity, too," she grumbled in a voice so low Brent wasn't sure it was intended to reach his ears.

He sighed. Shriveled up sounded a whole lot more appealing than being trampled. Though after the way Kayla hadn't given him so much as a wayward glance all morning, maybe it wouldn't come to that. Maybe she'd agree to help Ruby but give him the cold shoulder the rest of her stay. Then whatever appeal she had to him would slowly fade away.

Riiight.

Brent set his brush down at the edge of the tray, then stepped down off the ladder. All that reaching—reaching, not neck craning—had managed to put one hell of a kink in his back. He bent to stretch, then twisted slowly to the left and then to the right. A loud *pop* sounded in his lower back, and Brent felt instant relief.

Well, in his back anyway. Once his feet had hit the ground his anxiety level had spiked. Why was the idea of talking to Kayla—talking, not even something difficult like flirting or seducing—scaring him so badly?

Because maybe it's just not meant to be, said a voice in the back of his mind. The voice of doubt. Of fear.

The voice, he realized, he'd been listening to for far too long.

With a scowl he started forward, intent on breaking the silence. But as he rounded the corner of the building, Brent was surprised to see Kayla kneeling before a bed of daffodils, head bowed in an almost reverent gesture. Indecision slowed him to a stop. Maybe now wasn't the best time to try and talk to her after all.

But the clock was ticking—could he afford to wait?

Tuesday had gone from bad to worse for Kayla. First, she'd awoken all hot and bothered after a spicy dream involving her and a certain handyman, naked in the bed of his damned Silverado under a moonlit sky. Then, as if to add salt to that wound, she'd been stuck working within spitting distance of the hunky grouch. Thankfully, she had plenty of work to keep her busy. Too bad it had done little to silence her mind. Especially with the daffodils in bloom.

Oh, sure, she could stand to look at them in small doses. Could even stand to deadhead them once their lemon yellow blooms shriveled away. But having to mulch around bed after bed full of them? As much as she hated to admit it, the tears that clouded her vision late-morning spoke volumes.

Kayla still hadn't gotten over her mother's death. She doubted she ever would.

As she knelt upon the ground, clearing away a handful of last fall's leaves taking refuge beneath a cluster of daffodils, the tears that had been threatening for several minutes finally broke free from their bondage. She yanked off a glove and hurled it to the ground.

"Hey now," Brent said from somewhere close by. "What'd that glove ever do to you?"

"Nothing, it just...got in the way." Kayla swiped at her cheeks and kept her head turned from him. "So you can go back to painting the porch now."

Which, of course, he didn't do. Instead, his large frame drew closer and cast a shadow over where she knelt.

"Kayla?" The teasing tone in his voice had gone, replaced now by surprise and concern. He knelt down beside her and rested a hand on her shoulder. "Are you hurt?"

She shrugged out from under his touch and lifted her chin. "No. Please, just leave me alone."

He made no move to go. From the corner of her eye she saw him turn to look out over the sea of yellow before them. "You know, most people love daffodils. At least, that's what Ruby insisted when she made Miles and me plant a gazillion of them."

"Yeah, well, most people haven't been through what I have."

Brent reached out and tipped her chin in his direction. "Tell me."

The anger that had been so quick to surface yesterday was gone, his stormy gray eyes softened with concern. Concern for a woman who didn't deserve it, not from him or anyone else. She couldn't stay mad at Brent, not with him looking at her like that. It was almost like he cared about her, like he truly wanted to know what was wrong.

Like she mattered.

It'd been so long since anyone had looked at her in that way, since she'd *let* anyone get close enough to do so. Kayla felt an overwhelming need to comply, to tell him what had brought her to her knees. And yet, the notion of opening up scared her. Because opening up would unleash the grief she'd worked so hard to contain, to suppress.

But it had to be done if the healing was ever to follow, didn't it? Miles said Brent had dealt with his own grief. Of anyone she'd ever met, he might best be able to relate. It didn't make the task ahead any easier, though.

When she finally worked up the courage to speak, the words scratched at her throat like broken glass. "Daffodils were my mother's favorite flower. She loved to garden. Lived for it. When I was little, she'd take me to one of our local greenhouses each spring and steer me toward the annuals: petunias and marigolds, snapdragons and impatiens. She'd say, *Pick anything you like, sweetheart*, and set me loose. Once our cart was full, we'd head back home and spend the day planting.

"Well, *she* would spend the day planting. I usually got bored fairly quickly with the whole affair." An embarrassed grin tugged at her lips. "But not my mother. She would spend hour after hour out there. My father would bring her water or lemonade every hour or so, just to make sure she didn't shrivel up out in the sun."

Kayla could still picture her mother, kneeling before a flower bed, hands protected with pink gardening gloves and dirt smudges on her cheeks. She looked so much younger. So full of life. One whose days were unfairly numbered.

"Gardening was her joy, her passion. If she wasn't planting, she was pruning, or taking cuttings to bring inside. When the weather cooled in the fall and frost claimed the last of her blooms, she never complained. Instead, we'd venture to the home improvement stores and look for new varieties of bulbs to add to her collection. Daffodils, hyacinths, tulips, crocus—we always came away with something. Then we'd wait for a good planting day and head outside with a trowel and the bulbs. Mom would dig, I would drop bulbs into the holes. She showed me which end went up, and how to cover them just so. And then, we'd wait and see what happened next spring."

Kayla drew in a long, shaky breath as a familiar weight settled upon her chest.

"Eventually, though, I stopped caring so much about the flowers. The excitement wore off, and the planting rituals got in the way of me playing with my friends, or going out and doing my own thing. And then one day I woke up, and…"

She shook her head, wishing the gesture could sweep away the rest of the story. But of course, it couldn't. The guilt that weighed so heavily upon her was now joined with another emotion: regret.

"The call came spring of '08. My mother's gynecologist requested she come back in, something about test results not looking quite right. She'd been having some issues but never said anything to us kids. Didn't want us to worry. Tommy and I just assumed it was something minor. Cholesterol or blood sugar. But it wasn't, not even close. Within a week, the verdict was in: stage four ovarian cancer. The doctor said there aren't any standard tests for it, and since its symptoms mimic so many other problems, no one made the connection. We had no idea, no idea at all..." A small sob escaped her.

Brent pulled her onto his lap and held her close. For the first time in forever, she didn't try to resist sympathy or condolences. Instead she savored his warmth, his strength, as the tears flowed freely down her cheeks.

"I'm so sorry, Kayla."

"Mom fought it as best she could," Kayla whispered after a long moment. "They had her do chemo and radiation, which seemed to work for a while. But after a few months that type of chemo stopped holding the cancer at bay, so they went to a harsher cocktail. And a harsher one after that. Eventually, her body just couldn't take it any longer. She passed away the first week of December."

His arms tightened around her, and she felt Brent lower his cheek onto the top of her head. "She sounds like a true fighter. Something she clearly passed on to you."

"Thanks. I think." She felt Brent chuckle. "My mom was a believer, so I try to remind myself that she's in a better place now. That she's no longer hurting. But it doesn't make the pain go away."

"I know. It doesn't."

Kayla looked out over the bed of daffodils, their faces ever sunny, their scent intoxicating. "I'll never forget sitting on our couch, staring at a vase full of these darned flowers, when she told us about her terminal diagnosis. All I could think was would she be around long enough to plant them with me one last time? Or to see them bloom the next spring?"

Kayla clamped her eyes shut, wishing she could wipe that image from her mind and yet terrified someday the memory would fade. Because when that one faded away, the other memories of her mother would soon follow. Memories were all she had left.

All because she'd been so selfish.

"I took our time together for granted, Brent. Blew off our gardening traditions as I got older. If I'd spent more time with her, been there instead of being so self-absorbed, I might have picked up on her symptoms. Convinced her sooner to see the doctor, maybe bought her some more time—"

"Stop." Brent tipped Kayla's face up to his, then ran a thumb gently across each of her cheeks to wipe away the tears. "Thoughts like that will eat you alive. There was nothing you could have done to stop that cancer from happening. When it's your time, it's your time, and we just have to learn to accept that."

"Did you?"

He paused, his gaze wary. Would he close her off? Push her away? She hadn't meant to hurt him, to dredge up his own painful memories. She'd just been looking for, well, for *hope*.

"I see Miles has been shooting his mouth off again."

"Brent, I—"

"No, it's all right. He's always been better about talking about this than me." Brent sighed, then looked out over the sea of daffodils. "Did I learn to accept my parents' deaths? Yeah, I guess so. Do I still think it sucks, that it was unfair to them? To me? Yes. And I don't think that will ever change."

"I'm really sorry about your mom and dad," she said, and laced her arms around his waist.

"Thanks, me too." He rested his head atop hers and let out a long sigh. "You want me to mow over this flower bed for you? 'Cause if it'd make you feel better, I'd be more than happy to do it."

"What? No!" She pulled back and gave him a playful jab to the stomach. "No, I think I can do this now. Guess I just needed to get that off my chest."

"Well, if there's anything else you need help getting off—"

"Lunchtime!"

Kayla turned toward the sound of Ruby's voice and felt Brent's arms draw back from around her. She rose to her feet and leveled a stern look at him. "Now what were you starting to say?"

"Me? Nothin'." He winked, then bent to brush mulch from his jeans. "You'd better get inside, before your lunch gets cold."

"You're…not joining me? I mean us?"

He looked from her to the inn and back. "You wouldn't mind?"

"Only if you promise not to do any more yelling."

He studied her for a moment, as if waiting for her to change her mind. "I promise not to yell—with one exception."

"Oh? What's that?"

A slow grin stretched across his lips as he draped one arm over her shoulders. "If you ever even think of rooting for the Yankees."

Lord, that smile was swoon-worthy. And contagious. Kayla slid her arm around his waist to keep her balance as they started for the dining room.

"If that ever happens, you'd better yell *and* smack me."

"Oh, no. There's only room for one smack-happy pip-squeak around here," he said, ruffling her hair as they drew to a stop outside the back door. "And I think you've got that role covered."

"Darn straight," she mumbled, a fire lit in her cheeks. "So you just remember that."

"Oh, I will, princess." He pulled the door open and gestured for her to enter ahead of him. "I will."

Chapter Fifteen

Brent sat on his front porch Wednesday morning with a cup of joe in hand, watching the day chase away the night. It was another glorious sunrise, full of pinks and blues, and not a cloud in the sky. He drew in a deep breath of the humid, pine-scented air and tried to find peace. But peace had left him the moment he stepped into the path of one Kayla Daniels.

And he'd yet to find it since.

Every day—hell, every hour—since their accidental meeting on Friday had been an emotional roller coaster for him. The sight of her tugged at his carnal side, made his heart race and his libido spike. But it was her kind heart and giving nature that repeatedly drew him in and held him captive. Add in her musical voice and those unassuming beautiful blue eyes, and he was a goner.

At first, it'd pissed him off. He didn't want to be a goner, didn't want to feel, to want. But it seemed the harder he fought to push her away, the more determined fate was to thrust her right back into his arms. Except for Friday night, he'd more or less succeeded. Yesterday, though, had been the coup de grace.

Kayla had lost her mother to cancer. She was hurting, just like him.

It was rare to find people his age who'd experienced a loss similar to his. Most people didn't know what to say when the subject came up. They couldn't relate to his pain, his misery. Over time, he'd learned to bottle it up. To keep it out of conversations entirely.

It was easier that way for everyone involved. Or, at least, that's what he'd grown to believe.

When Kayla sat with him yesterday, in desperate need of someone to listen and comfort her while she poured her heart out about the loss of her own mother, it'd caught him completely off-guard. He wasn't used to talking about loss, let alone offering advice on the subject. She'd asked him if he'd come to accept his parents' deaths.

Until that moment, Brent hadn't realized that he had.

He drew in another deep breath, then slowly released it. The weight on his shoulders felt lighter somehow today, as though the knowledge that he'd achieved even a minimal amount of healing brought with it a lessening of the burden he'd long carried. A knowledge that he might not have come to discover for who knows how long had it not been for Kayla.

Bear gave up on tracking the animal that had long since skedaddled, and moseyed his way up onto the porch. He stopped before Brent, lowered his hindquarters onto the floor, then set his massive jowls in Brent's lap.

"You miss her, don't you, boy?"

Bear looked up at him, his eyebrows shifting in a silent admission. Brent ran his free hand over Bear's head and rubbed behind his ears. For his efforts, he was rewarded with a quick, sloppy kiss to the hand.

"Yeah, I kinda miss her, too. Guess I ought to get used to it, though."

Bear scooted closer, crowding Brent's legs with his own.

"She's not from around here, Bear. And I can't do long-distance relationships."

The pup dug his nose into the side of Brent's leg.

"Yeah, you're right—I can't do any relationships. Which is why I have you."

Brent offered his dog a halfhearted grin. He loved his four-legged roommate. But this morning, for the first time in forever, he felt the need for more. For companionship of the two-legged variety. His gaze shifted back to the sunrise, its glow brightening the skies from pinks and lavenders to a fiery orange. The view lit something inside of him with an emotion he hadn't felt in far too long.

Hope.

Maybe it was time he stop fighting fate and let the cards fall where they may. He might not have forever with Kayla but, as far as he knew, he still had today. Sure, he'd already planned to stick close to her, to see if he couldn't talk her into helping come up with some advertising tricks that might help him save the inn. But now, as he sat on his porch, a lonely man with his dog, Brent couldn't help but wonder if the inn wasn't the only thing needing saving.

And if Kayla might be the one who could save them both.

Kayla hit the flower beds first thing Wednesday morning. It was either that or stare at her computer, willing emails to appear. After staying up into the wee hours of the night crafting the perfect angle with which to approach the Follinger project, she thought it would be a struggle to wake up. But instead of having to drag herself out of bed she'd sprung out, dying to know if anyone from her team had gone in early and seen the proposal.

Of course, no one had. She'd held the position of "team member with no life" for years; why would this week be any different? But instead of being discouraged by the radio silence, she chose to keep her chin up. They would get to work, be wowed by her research and suggestions, and dive in to crafting the perfect bid proposal.

And it was perfect. Not even that smug little twerp Joe Freimann would be able to refute it. To hear him admit that, to watch him squirm beneath the weight of his stepfather's scowl when his assured subpar proposal was placed next to hers, would almost be worth a week off with no pay.

Almost.

For now, though, she needed to get some work done outside to earn her keep at the inn. The air around her was cool, and a sheer blanket of dew lay across the Checkerberry's broad green lawn. In the distance, birds chirped their happy springtime songs, and chipmunks chattered. Kayla stood beside the inn, wishing there were a way to bottle up the moment and save it somehow. Then, when she was back in Fort Wayne and stuck behind her desk on some gloomy, stressful day, she could uncork the bottle and let Michigan's natural beauty soothe her frayed nerves.

"Lollygagging already?" Brent asked, appearing out of nowhere.

Kayla jumped, then felt her pulse quicken. He had that effect on her, every time.

"No, I was savoring the moment." She swatted at him with her empty garden gloves, but he was quick on his feet and easily dodged her strike. "'Was' being the key word."

"There's plenty more where this comes from when you live around here." Brent sucked in a deep breath, his sandstone T-shirt stretching tight against his chest as he did so. Not that Kayla noticed. Much. He exhaled then threw her a smirk. "Nope, none of that city smog stinking up our air."

Kayla laughed. "I live in Fort Wayne, Brent, not Detroit. We don't have smog. At least, not on my side of town. Though it's not nearly so peaceful in the city this time of day."

"Pretty noisy there, is it?"

She looked up to study him. Why so much interest in where she lived all of a sudden? "It can be. Especially when you live in an apartment. You never know what your neighbors will be up to at any given moment."

"Something tells me I wouldn't do so well as an apartment dweller."

"Why's that?"

"Because I like my sleep. If someone started blaring their stereo at odd hours of the night, it'd probably come to blows between us."

The image of him lying on his back beside her, naked and spent from their moonlight activities Friday invaded her thoughts without invitation. She'd managed to stay awake a few minutes longer than he had and had just stared at him, fascinated. Asleep, his face softened and took on a youthful, almost angelic look. But awake…

Well, she'd seen his ticked off, not-so-angelic looks, too.

With a shake of her head, she pushed the memories aside. "Yeah, I guess not everyone's cut out for city life."

Brent stood beside her, his gaze sweeping the yard. Heat rolled off his body, chasing away the chill in the air around them. Kayla found herself wanting to lean in closer and soak up some of that warmth. But that wouldn't help her get the landscaping done any faster, and she was already itching to get back inside and check her email inbox.

"You sick of playing in the petunias yet?"

She looked up, surprised by how close he'd come to reading her thoughts. "Um, no. Since there aren't any petunias out here."

"I could order some, to keep you busy—"

"No!"

Brent grinned. "That's what I thought. How about you work for a bit and then come find me? Once I finish this first coat of paint, I've got another task I could use your help on."

"My help? Wait, did big, bad Brent Masterson really just ask the pipsqueak for help?"

He leaned in closer, the delicious scent of his clean yet spicy aftershave washing over her. "Maybe he did. But if you tell anyone, he'd have to kill you."

"I'd like to see him try."

A wicked grin stretched across his lips. "Feisty this morning. I like it. Hang on to those emotions, princess. They might come in handy later."

With that he smacked her on the ass. On the ass! Kayla

whirled around to take another swing at him with her gloves, but he'd already jogged out of reach.

"It's a good thing you're quicker than you are smart," she called, her butt still stinging.

"It's a good thing you're…well, we'll see."

We'll see? Kayla planted a fist on each hip, ready for the verbal jabs to continue, but Brent just chuckled as he rounded the porch without another look back.

Oh, he was up to something. What it was, she had no idea. But between his kind words and playful demeanor yesterday and today's all out flirting, the grouch had transformed into Mr. Charming.

And darn it if that smile didn't make her melt every single time he flashed it her way. Earlier in the week, she would have kept her distance, maybe even hidden from him. Today, his outgoing nature was gearing up to be the perfect distraction to her work anxiety.

Why not have a little fun and run with it?

B rent had never rolled a coat of paint so fast in his life. Mainly because he'd never had a reason to before now. Painting was a hurry-up-and-wait kind of task. And watching paint dry was about as exciting as, well, watching paint dry.

But not today. Today he had other activities lined up. Activities that would take him and Kayla away from the inn and give them some time alone—away from work, away from meddling family members, and away from their pain.

He could hardly stand the wait.

"Hey, Green Thumb!" He called as he walked around

back to the tool shed. "You about done over there?"

Kayla looked up from a flower bed that sat between the pool and parking areas and smiled. God, she was beautiful when she did that.

"Five more minutes?"

"Perfect. Gives me time to wash up. You need anything before we head out? A sandwich or something?"

"Head out?" She stood and brushed mulch from her knees. "Where exactly is this project of yours?"

"*Projects*. The first, though, is down by the pond."

Her smile faded. "Oh. Um, no, I'm not hungry yet. But I should probably head inside and hit the restroom before we go."

"Sure. Why don't you do that, and meet me back out here when you're ready. That is, if you're not—"

"If you call me chicken one more time, Brent, so help me—"

Relief washed over him as her wary look turned back to the stubborn one he'd grown to adore. A little more taunting was sure to solidify her decision. "I was going to say too tired to go. But if you're afraid to enter the woods with me…"

"Of course not."

Her chin jutted up, and Brent was glad he had his hands full of paint supplies. Otherwise he'd have been tempted to close the distance between them and cup that chin in his hands to hold her still for one long, satisfying kiss.

"Okay, but don't take too long. I haven't got all day." *And I want as much time with you as I can get before fate steals you away.*

He continued on to the shed and caught the faint sound of her mumbling under her breath—something about him being bossy. Oh, yeah, he'd love to get bossy with her. But not here, not out in the open. No, he'd love to take control in the bedroom, when it was just the two of them. Bring her to her knees with want, need. Though one pout from those perfect pink lips and he'd relinquish control. Gladly.

Brent headed inside a few minutes later, distracted by a fantasy that included Kayla on her knees looking up at him with a naughty grin, when he nearly collided with his grandmother.

"Oh!" Ruby's hand flew to her chest. "Goodness, Brent, you gave me such a fright."

"Sorry." Guilt and embarrassment warmed his cheeks. "You okay?"

"I will be in a moment."

"Here, why don't you sit, let your heart rate slow down?"

He put a hand on her shoulder and tried to guide her toward the nearest chair in the dining room, but she waved him off.

"I'm old, but I'm not that old."

Brent chuckled. "Well, at least I know your sense of humor is still intact."

"Apparently, so is yours." A knowing grin stretched slowly across her soft, wrinkled face. "Things are going well today, I see?"

"Yep, got the first coat rolled on the porch."

"I wasn't talking about the porch," she said.

"And I'm not talking about anything but."

The two stood toe-to-toe, arms crossed and gazes locked. Masterson stubbornness at its finest. Her wise old eyes narrowed.

"You've cleaned up."

"Maybe I'm done painting for a while."

"Shall I pack a lunch for you two?"

"I—" Damn it, how did she *know* these things? "That would be great, thank you."

A smug grin tugged at her lips once more. "I'll be sure to pack strawberries. Though I don't have any champagne on hand."

"Jesus, Ruby. It's lunch, not a proposal."

"Language," she warned. "And maybe not. Yet."

She walked off, a swagger to her step, leaving a suddenly terrified Brent in her wake.

Not yet? Oh, God. He hadn't thought that far ahead, hadn't pictured what the future might hold if he did put his heart on the line. Last time, it'd ended badly. Very badly. This time…

He shook his head. *It's just lunch, remember, dummy?* No reason to get caught up in Ruby's mind games. Kayla was funny and smart, adorably stubborn, and yeah, he was dying to get her naked body beneath him again. But they were a light year away from anything permanent, and it would be best for him to remember that. Especially if he wanted to keep his heart intact when the time came for her to leave.

Chapter Sixteen

Kayla headed inside after finishing with that last flower bed and kicked her dirty shoes off by the inn's back door—no sense in making anyone do extra cleaning on her behalf. Or maybe she could make a mess and then volunteer to clean it up. Might help keep her away from the pond.

Of all the places he could have picked to ask for help.

With a frown she headed upstairs. He'd probably laugh at her if he knew she couldn't swim, or that the mere mention of any significant body of water made the hairs on the back of her neck stand upright. She'd just have to play it cool and hope like heck they wouldn't go anywhere near the water. Maybe there was a picnic table in dire need of repair, or a little shed that needed to be re-shingled.

She'd take heights over water any day.

A quick check of her inbox soon had her forgetting all about the water, though. Six emails awaited, all from different staff members on her team and all very excited. She plunked down in front of her laptop and quickly answered their questions and offered a bit more direction. Unfortunately, what felt like a minute had turned into ten. Brent was sure to be pacing by now.

With a sigh, she closed her machine, hit the bathroom, and headed downstairs. In truth, there wasn't much more she could do from here now, so the outing with Brent couldn't have come at a better time. Though with the way he'd been acting of late, she would have to keep her guard up. Who knew what that man was up to?

Kayla slipped her shoes back on and headed out the door. Brent sat in the Gator's driver's seat, drumming his fingers on the steering wheel. *Not big on patience, this one*, she thought with a grin.

"Oh, good. I was beginning to think you'd drowned in there. Nearly called 911."

"Sorry, had to squeeze in a little work."

He frowned. "I thought you were off this week."

"Well, technically." She took a seat beside him and shrugged. "But I think I found a surefire way to get my boss to overlook Friday's little incident."

"If he does, he sure as hell better pay you for your time off, too."

Brent's voice was low and menacing as he steered them for the barn. Not exactly the mood she'd hoped he would be in this afternoon. No, what she'd been hoping for was a lot more smiling. Maybe even him getting all hot and sweaty and needing to take his shirt off, giving her another peek at those amazing abs of his.

"Well, if he doesn't, would you drive down there and beat him up for me?" She threw him a grin—it had been her daydream since the moment she first saw him, after all.

He looked at her in surprise for a moment, then shook his head and chuckled. "Wow. Groundskeeper, hit man—I'm building up one heck of a resume here."

"*Pfft*, like you need one. Ruby will never fire you."

"Not unless she has to."

"Has to? Why would— Oh. You mean if the inn closed?"

Brent nodded. "Yeah. Ruby thinks we'll be fine, but Miles…well, Miles isn't so sure. Truth is, I think he's already putting out feelers, trying to see if there's any interest in buying the place."

"Oh, I sure hope not. I mean, I've never actually seen it open, but it's so quiet and peaceful right now. Not noisy and crowded like normal hotels."

"It gets a little noisier with more guests here, but not by much. People come to relax, to get away from work and stress and whatever else is plaguing them."

He was quiet for a moment, intent on the trail that wound down around the barn and out into the woods beyond. Ruby had taken Kayla down this same path on Monday, but the mood this trip was far more melancholy. She wished there were something she could do to help. There was no doubt Ruby loved this place—it shone in her every gesture and word.

"What we need is a way to draw people back to the Checkerberry, help them rediscover the road less traveled, you know?"

"Do you guys have a website?"

Brent shrugged. "Yes, but it probably hasn't been updated in a while. In fact, I don't know that anyone's even touched it since we hired our chef Maddie, and that's been a few years."

"Oh, wow. Yeah, you're probably missing out big time there. If Maddie's half as talented as you all say she is, you could be advertising her menus. Draw people here just for the meals, and when they fall in love with the atmosphere, they'll spread the word."

He grinned.

"What?" she asked.

"Nothing. The website update sounds like a great idea, but I don't know how much money we have in the budget for that."

"It might not cost all that much, actually," she said. "Especially with Central Michigan being right here in Mount Pleasant. You could probably get some college kid to do the changes pretty cheap."

"Maybe. Though wouldn't an ad in the paper be better? Miles said you gave him a few pointers on one he'd been toying with."

"I did. Has he sent it off yet?"

"Lord, I hope not. Did you not take a close enough look at the thing? Bear could have done better."

Kayla laughed. "It wasn't *that* bad."

Brent threw her a flat look.

"Yeah, all right, it was. But yes, I gave him some pointers that should have helped clean up a lot of it. I haven't seen a finished product yet, though, so who knows what the final version will look like. And honestly? People don't read the paper looking for ads like that. They look online. Advertise on a travel site and I bet you'd strike gold."

"Not with Miles's chicken scratch we won't. What we need is a professional's touch, someone who knows this place well and has an eye for this kind of thing."

And there it was—the reason he'd been so nice to her the past day. Dang it, she should have known. Kayla curled her hands into fists and looked away, trying to keep her temper under control. Why? Why did everyone she meet feel the need to take advantage of her giving heart?

No more.

"Stop the cart."

B rent slowed the Gator to a stop at Kayla's demand. "What's wrong? Did we forget something?"

"Nope." She climbed out of her seat and started back the way they'd come.

"Then where are you going?"

"Back. I'm going back, where I should have stayed all along."

Shit. This wasn't how he wanted the day to go. Brent jumped out and jogged after her.

"Kayla wait. *Wait.*" He snagged her arm, but she refused to meet his gaze.

"I'm done, Brent. Done letting people take advantage of me."

"What are you talking about?" But he already knew and felt terrible about it. He never should have listened to Miles. Then again, had Miles not planted the crazy idea in his head to ask her for help, he wouldn't have allowed himself to get close to her yesterday. And she'd needed him, almost as much as he'd needed her.

Her healing had become his own. And he'd be damned if he was going to tuck tail and run so soon.

She tugged free of his grip. "Really? I mean, really? You act all nice to me, let me cry on your freaking shoulder, and then drive me out here and just happen to mention that you could use some cheap help with advertising?"

"I'm not *acting* nice. There is never butt-swatting involved in acting nice. And that's not why I brought you out here."

"Oh, yeah? Why'd you bring me out here then, huh?"

His body moved faster than his brain. Suddenly he had her in his arms, his lips on hers. Kayla's body went rigid with surprise. She pressed both hands to his chest, but he pulled her closer and deepened the kiss.

The hands on his chest softened…then collected two fistfuls of his shirt. Her sweet lips parted, and then it was her tongue seeking his. He opened to her, allowed her to roam, to explore. Her hand slid to cup the back of his neck and she pulled Brent closer. A shiver of delight rippled through him.

Kayla's lips tugged into a grin over his. She nipped at his lower lip, then pulled back as though her conscience had finally caught up with her actions. Brent wrapped his arms around her, unwilling to let go just yet. Hell, if she promised to kiss him like that every day he might never release her.

The thought both startled and scared him. He tipped his forehead to hers and waited for his pulse to slow. "I'm sorry for upsetting you."

"Yeah, well, I might have overreacted a tiny bit. It's just…I stink at sticking up for myself. But you." She shook her head. "You bring out a whole other side of me. The feisty side."

Brent bent to kiss in the hollow beneath her ear. "I kinda like feisty."

"I can tell." Her breathy answer had him hard as a rock. "But, um, didn't you say you were on a tight schedule?"

"Schedule? What schedule?" He traced her ear with his nose. It was her turn to shiver.

"Brent…"

He sighed. She was right, of course. Didn't make getting back to work suck any less.

"Fine." He released her and looked toward the Gator, then to Kayla. "You coming, or you heading back?"

"If I go with you, you'll probably just tick me off again."

Disappointment flared in his chest. Damn, he'd been sure she enjoyed the kiss as much as he had. He turned to go and gave himself a solid mental kick. *This* was why he didn't put himself out there. Always with the disappointment.

"Then again," she said. "I kinda hope you do."

He looked back. "What?"

"Well, you know." She threw him a deviously flirty look. "I rather enjoy the whole making up part."

He watched that tight little ass of hers sashay its way back to the Gator. She resumed her seat, then turned to offer him a "come hither" look. Brent took a few deep breaths, to keep from doing just that…and then ravishing her right there in the front seat.

God, she was going to be his undoing. Trouble was, the more time he spent with her, the more open to the idea he became. He was falling for her, hard. But would he be able to pull out of the tailspin that was sure to follow her return to Indiana?

Then again, if she didn't go back, there wouldn't be a tailspin, now would there? Brent swallowed hard. His workload had just increased for the day, only this time the new task involved a muscle he didn't typically let get involved at work.

His heart.

Chapter Seventeen

Once Brent knew he could walk without hurting himself, he closed the distance between them and slid into the driver's seat. After a moment Kayla looked away from the trail to flash him a smile. It wasn't quite as devious as the one she'd tossed him a moment before, but hey, at least it was a smile. Now if he could just keep her smiling, maybe she'd start to let him into her heart, too.

"This work down at the pond," she said once they were moving again. "We don't actually have to go in the water, do we?"

"I sure as hell hope not. This early in the season, the water's still ice cold."

"Oh. Good."

"Not a big fan of water?"

"I'm fine with water. Perfectly fine. Why would I not be? I mean, who doesn't love water?"

Oh yeah, she's afraid all right. "How about I promise to

do my best to keep you dry? Will that work?"

"Um, yeah." The pond came into view, and her gaze grew wary. "So, what was it you needed to do down here, anyway?"

"Well, we've had unusually wet springs the past few years, which means the pond has been sitting higher, longer. Since we don't take the pier out for winter, it got submerged a few times. Sped up the deterioration process. Now we've got a couple boards that look like they're starting to rot. Ruby's worried about people walking on them and falling through or something." He parked the Gator a short distance from the pier and climbed out.

"Wouldn't want that," Kayla mumbled, eyes on the pier and frozen in her seat.

"Look, all we need to do is pry up four or five boards and then screw the new ones into place."

"New boards," she echoed. Her eyes brightened. "Oh, so we'll need to cut the new boards? And stain them? I could do that for you. The tools are back at the barn, right?"

"Nope, I measured the boards last week. Cut and stained them over the weekend." Brent walked around and stopped before her, blocking her view of the pier. "All I need you to do is play nurse while I operate. Hand me tools, boards, screws…"

Kayla's right brow arched higher on her forehead. Oops, so that'd been a bit of a Freudian slip. Not that he'd ever turn her away from playing nurse or offering screws.

One thing at a time, Masterson…

"You think you can handle that?"

Her eyes narrowed. "Of course I can handle it."

"Good."

A bee buzzed past his ear, and Brent pushed the whole nurse thing aside—temporarily. DeWalt cordless drill in hand, he headed for the pier. Kayla, however, remained in the Gator, white-knuckling the seat cushion.

"Gonna be difficult to hand me supplies from way over there."

"I-I'm enjoying the view, all right?"

"If you say so."

Brent grinned and kept walking. If there was one thing he'd learned being around Kayla, it was that she couldn't resist a battle of the wills. He stepped out onto the pier and stopped at the first rotten board he came to. Too bad it was a good ten feet out from shore—she probably wouldn't come anywhere near this far. He flipped the DeWalt's direction switch to reverse.

"So how long have you lived in Fort Wayne?"

"My whole life," she called. "My parents, too. Tommy was the first rebel, chose an out-of-state college."

"Your dad stayed there, then?"

"Oh, yeah. Too many memories he'd have to leave behind."

"I can understand that." Brent cast a quick glance back at the Gator. Kayla had still made no move to leave her seat. Wow, she really was afraid of the water. *Best to keep her talking then.* Another bee buzzed by as he knelt down on the pier. "Is that why you stayed, too?"

"No. I stayed because I had a year of college left. And then I got a job offer from Wayne Advertising right after graduation."

Brent set about loosening the screws from the rotten plank. Once they were nearly out, he stopped with the drill and loosened them the rest of the way by hand to keep them from falling into the pond. With his luck, he'd be the one to step on them this summer and need a damned tetanus shot. "Can't beat that. Was it the first job you'd applied for?"

"No. But it was the only company where my dad had connections."

"Ah. Well, you know what they say—it's not what you know, it's who you know who knows who you need to know."

Kayla laughed. "Wow, say that five times really fast." Her mood sobered then. "Unfortunately, it's turned out to be more of a curse than a blessing. I'm starting to think I'd rather be hired for what I know, not because of who knows whom."

"Never underestimate connections, Kayla," Brent said, freeing the last old screw. "You never know when one might come in handy."

He stood, tucked the loose screws into his back pocket, then straddled the loose plank. "You ready to help me?" he asked, looking at his still-seated helper.

Her gaze flickered to the pond.

"I promise to keep you dry," he said, his voice low and sure.

"You already said that." Her eyes narrowed as she stepped out of the Gator.

He shrugged. "Seemed like something worth repeating. Now, here's how this is going to work. I'm going to pull up the old boards one at a time and bring them to you. You throw them in the back of the Gator and then bring me a new one. Got it?"

"Got it. Oh!" Kayla swatted at something near her face. "I wouldn't have expected bees to be out this early in the season."

"Well, don't swat at it, you'll only piss it off."

She bobbed again and took a few hurried steps toward the edge of the pier. "Give me the board already, will you?"

Brent rolled his eyes. Darned city girl. He stepped forward, knelt down by the pier's side, and grabbed hold of the board's edge that he'd just loosened. If he was lucky, the entire piece would come free without snapping. Though judging by how badly rotted the piece was, he didn't expect that to happen. He gave the board a careful tug. It didn't move.

"Huh," he said, glancing back to make sure he'd removed all the screws holding it to the pier. Which, as far as he could tell, he had.

"What, forget to eat your Wheaties this morning?"

"Wheaties are nasty," he grumbled, and gave the board another tug. Still nothing. Two bees buzzed by. "And they're missing a key ingredient."

"What's that?"

"Bacon."

Brent tightened his grip once more and gave the board a solid jerk. Still nothing. Pissed that it wouldn't budge, he stood and straddled the rotten plank, then reached down with both hands.

"Right," said Kayla. "Because growing boys need their—"

Brent gave the board a mighty tug, and a section of it broke free. Attached to its underside was part of a massive, formerly hidden beehive. In an instant the air around him came alive as an angry swarm of bees blotted out the sun and drowned out whatever Kayla was saying. Brent dropped the plank and scrambled backward. Three steps later, his foot met thin air.

Kayla watched in horror as a cloak of angry bees seemed to swallow Brent whole. Her fears intensified when, in a desperate attempt to flee the buzzing monsters, he stumbled right off the pier and into the pond.

"Brent!" She screamed, and ran along the shoreline away from the pier, eyes focused on the water's surface. "Brent!"

Oh, God, where is he?

The swarm of bees condensed over the pier, the buzz nearly deafening. Even if Kayla could swim, there'd be no way for her to dive in from there and save him without getting stung a thousand times. No, the only way to save him now would be by swimming out to where he'd gone in.

Only, she couldn't swim.

"No, no, no!" she cried, hands on either side of her head. She couldn't bear to stand there, helpless, watching him drown. In a panic she rushed forward, stopping at the edge of the water.

How hard can it be? Paddle with my arms, kick with my legs. Ripples from his splash lapped at the shore, taunting her.

But common sense quickly wove its way back into her consciousness. She had no idea how deep the water was, or how she'd ever manage to pull him to shore without drowning herself. That's when she saw a line of bubbles in the water, running parallel with the shore a dozen feet or so out. A second later, Brent broke through the surface, gasping for air.

"Brent! Oh, thank God. Swim this way, over here."

His gaze flashed to the buzzing pier, then back to her. "A-a-are y-you al-l r-right?"

"Me?" Kayla stared at him, dumbfounded. What kind of stupid question was that? "I'm fine. Now get out of there before you catch hypothermia."

"H-hypo-th-thermia's n-n-not s-something you c-c-catch."

With a grunt, Brent pushed against something beneath him, and Kayla watched him rise out of the pond. He started toward the shore, the water skimming his upper thighs.

"Wait, *that's* how deep it is over there? Of all the… Do you know how worried I was that you were going to *drown*?"

A faint grin came to his lips, which, she noticed as he drew closer, had taken on a bluish tint. "P-people have d-drowned in less." Brent's gaze shifted back to the pier as he sloshed his way out. "C-can't believe I d-didn't s-see the d-damned hive."

"There was no way you could have. The cattails block the view from shore."

He stood before her now, soaking wet and shivering, water running off him and dripping to the ground like a soft, spring rain.

"How badly did you get stung?"

"N-not sure. C-can't feel much. T-too c-cold."

"Crap, you are going to go into hypothermia." She hurried toward the Gator and started riffling through its back cart. "Don't you have a jacket or something in here?"

"Ruby p-packed a blanket," he managed. "F-for the p-picnic lunch."

"Well, you won't have much need for lunch if you go into

shock and stop breathing." She located a patchwork quilt packed alongside the cooler and snatched it up, then hurried over to Brent and threw it around his shoulders. "Better?"

"S-sure." A spasm rocked through him, and he nearly lost his balance.

"You're a terrible liar, Brent Masterson. Come on, we need to get you out of those wet clothes."

His right brow arched, and Kayla's mouth went dry. "Not here," she managed to grind out. "Now get in, I'm driving."

"F-fine," he said. "B-but not to R-Ruby's. We're going t-to my p-place."

"We don't have time to drive all the way over there. You need to get dry before the rest of you turns blue. Or pneumonia sets in! And you probably need to see a doctor. Who knows how many times you got stung?"

"No," he growled, and stumbled into the Gator's passenger seat. "And I d-don't need a d-damned doctor. I j-just need a hot s-shower and some d-dry clothes."

"You aren't allergic to bee stings, are you?" Kayla jumped into the driver's seat and stomped on the gas. The Gator didn't move. "Oh, God, please don't be allergic to bee stings. How far is it to the nearest hospital? What if we can't make it in time?" She slammed her hand on the Gator's dash. "And what is *wrong* with this thing?"

"Kayla, s-stop." Brent's hand touched her shoulder, his voice calm. "It's going to b-be all right. My h-house is on the other side of those w-woods. It's q-quicker than going back to the inn, and I n-need dry clothes."

She stared up at him, wanting to believe the sureness in his stormy gray eyes. But his lips…they were definitely blue. Could the Gator really get them to his place in time?

"T-trust me." He reached up and placed his hand on her cheek.

There he was, ice cold and shivering to beat the band yet trying to comfort *her*. But why? Why was he so worried about her?

Because he cared.

Oh, no. No, this couldn't be happening. She hadn't meant to lead him on, didn't want to break his heart the way his ex-fiancée Nikki had.

I should never have kissed him like that in the woods.

Guilt weighed on her so heavily she wanted to scream. Instead, she drew in a deep breath and focused on doing the responsible thing: take him home and make sure he was okay. After that, well, she'd have to think of a way to let him down easy. Because if things were gearing up back at work like she thought, then her time here was short. Indiana was waiting.

"Fine. Which way to your place?"

Chapter Eighteen

A hot shower never felt so good, and never smarted so bad. Kayla had refused to let Brent leave her sight once they arrived at his place; she'd followed him upstairs and insisted on inspecting him for bee stings. He shooed her out of his master bathroom once the shower was running, refusing to have her see him shiver and shake his way out of his sopping wet clothes. Once they were off, he lunged for the shower, eager for reprieve from the cold…and having forgotten just how damned painful a hot shower on a cold body could be.

He roared as the lukewarm water rained down on his body, turning his bluish skin instantly to red.

"Is it still too hot?" Her voice was laced with concern.

No way would he fess up to that, especially after it'd been her idea to dial it back from the scalding temperature he'd first selected. Brent worked to keep his temper, and his chattering teeth, in check. "N-no."

"Okay."

Another spasm rippled through Brent's body. He'd never been submerged in water so cold before. Hoped to never be again. The bathroom door squeaked open.

"You doing all right? Because if you are, I could get these clothes in the wash for you."

Brent sighed. The woman had gone into Energizer Bunny mode after his plunge in the pond, always moving or talking. Or both. "F-first floor, behind the kitchen."

"Great. I'll be right back. Oof! Yes, Bear, you can come, too."

The door closed behind her, and a blessed silence descended upon the room. Brent turned the water temp up a notch and bit back a cry of pain. Damn, it stung. But not as much as his pride. Right now, he didn't know which was worse—falling into the pond in front of Kayla, or barely being able to make it upstairs from all the shivering and muscle cramps. And if she insisted on a clinical full-body inspection after his shower, well, that might just kill him.

What a mess.

He closed his eyes and felt the burning sensation start to ease from his skin. Kayla had been in a total panic back by the pond. Insisting they get him to a hospital, that he needed to see a doctor. She'd done that with his hand after the fight at Chevvy's, too. What was with her always thinking he needed to get to a doctor, anyway?

Then it dawned on him: her mother.

Only the doctors hadn't been able to save Mrs. Daniels. Her illness had fallen outside the usual range of tests, had gone undetected. It must have been hell for Kayla, to watch the cancer eat away the woman she clearly looked up to. But still, her mother hadn't been taken overnight, she hadn't had to learn of her death from a detached police investigator.

God, what he would have given for some advance notice of that plane crash. A chance to tell his parents good-bye, to let them know how much he loved them...

"You still doing okay in there?"

Kayla's voice woke him from his silent pity party. "Uh, yeah. Starting to thaw out."

"Great!"

The hot water began to cool, and Brent knew his time was up. *Damn.* He shut the water off.

"Done already?"

"Old water heater, doesn't hold much. Guess it's time to update." Brent moved to the far end of the shower and reached a hand out from behind the curtain. "Towel, please?"

A warm, soft towel met his hand. Fresh from the dryer? He hugged it to his chest and savored its warmth and the scent of his favorite fabric softener. She had no idea how much the gesture meant to him right now.

"I found some baking soda while I was downstairs and made up a paste for any stings we find. Hopefully there won't be any stingers still in there — I hate trying to pry those suckers out."

Brent grimaced at the thought. "Thanks. Why don't you just leave that stuff on the counter, and I'll take care of it when I'm done?"

"Nice try, buddy. But unless you grew a set of eyes in the back of your head, you're gonna need my help. Besides, you aren't really going to play shy with me, are you? I have seen you without your clothes on before."

"Says the woman who's still fully clothed."

"Yes. And you should know, she plans to stay that way."

A devious grin tugged at his lips. Her voice had waivered on that last sentence. No waiver meant no chance, but that sound? *Hmm, maybe being naked isn't such a bad thing after all…*

Brent put the towel to his face and drew in a deep breath. He hadn't had a chance to tell his parents how he felt before they were gone. Was he really going to stand there and do the same thing with Kayla? Because he was definitely falling for her—that warm towel had just pushed him right over the edge. If only he could convince her to give him a chance, to leave Indiana and all that stress and heartache.

"Do you need help drying off?"

"You in a hurry to see me naked or what?" He grinned at the prospect.

"No. I need to make sure you're not a walking bee stinger pincushion."

"Uh-huh."

Brent gingerly dragged the towel back and forth across his back. So far, so good. Oh hell, good nothing—it was a freaking miracle he wasn't covered in stings from head to toe. The cooler weather had saved his ass. That, and the freezing water. He did a quick inspection of his lower extremities. Nope, no stings visible.

"You know, if you did get stung you're gonna want to get this paste on before the itching gets too bad."

He tucked the towel loosely around his waist, pushed the curtain back, and leveled a look of mock annoyance at her as he stepped out of the shower. Kayla's gaze fixed on his naked torso and her cheeks blossomed with pink.

She cleared her throat and stepped behind him. "Now,

uh, just hold still while I check you out."

"You know, usually when people check each other out, they don't give a play by play."

"This isn't that kind of checking you out."

He grinned at her insolent tone. "Find anything back there?"

"So far, only two stings on each shoulder blade, no stingers visible. Man, I can't believe how lucky you were." She dabbed some of the cold goop onto his shoulder. "Do they itch?"

He sucked in a sharp breath as the cold paste met his skin. "No. Maybe I'm still in shock or something."

The thought only worried him slightly. Right now, he had more important things on his mind. Like how best to take advantage of their tight quarters.

"God, I hope not. It's been too long since I took a CPR class. I don't even remember what to do with someone who's gone into shock."

"Tsk, tsk, tsk. And you call yourself a nurse."

"No. I don't." She lifted his arm and inspected the left side of his body. "And besides, I'd make a terrible nurse. I... don't do well in hospitals."

Brent watched her work, enjoying that she was too focused on looking for embedded stingers to notice him staring. Kayla's brows were pulled into a small V as she chewed on her lower lip. She looked absolutely adorable, concentrating like that. Good thing she wasn't a nurse — who knows how many patients she'd have hitting on her.

She ducked behind him again, brushed her hand gently across his back, and lifted his other arm.

"Find anything else?" he asked.

"Not so far."

"You know," he said, hamming it up. "I think I'm starting to feel a sting."

"You do?" Kayla lowered his arm. "Where?"

"On my face." She moved to stand before him, that damned bowl of paste in her hands. How could he get her to put it down? "Above my left eye. Do you see it?"

"No. Where?"

He raised a hand to point to his left brow, careful to keep the other hand clamped onto the top edge of his towel.

"I…I don't see anything," Kayla said, her gaze intent on where he was pointing. "Bend down a little."

He did, but only a tiny bit. With a sigh, she set the bowl aside and placed a hand on each of his shoulders, pulling him down to eye level. Her lips were only a whisper away from his. "I still don't see—"

"Don't you?" Brent's eyes drifted shut as he drew in a breath and savored her scent. Lilac and vanilla. He wet his lips. "Maybe you're not looking hard enough."

"Well, I don't know how I could miss it this close up."

"Me, either." Brent leaned forward and claimed her mouth with his own. All his worries about stings and shock and last good-byes vanished in an instant.

Kayla froze.

What was Brent doing, kissing her *now*? After he'd just had a near-death experience? Maybe he really was going into shock. Kayla pulled back, breaking the kiss, and ignored the way every neuron in her body threatened to rebel.

"I'm not done," she said, as much for herself as for him.

"Sure you are." His voice was low. And seductive. Far too seductive.

Could someone in shock sound like that?

Kayla put a hand on his chest to stop him from stealing a second kiss. His solid, warm chest. She swallowed hard. "Wait."

"Why?"

He pushed her hand aside and leaned in for another kiss. Kayla turned her face, but Brent simply changed targets. His mouth grazed her jawline and slid down to the hollow beneath her ear. A shudder rippled through her body as his warm breath tickled her neck.

"Because clearly you're going into shock. How far is it to the nearest clinic?"

"I told you, I'm fine." His free hand reached up and tugged at her ponytail. Her chin tipped up, leaving her neck exposed. Brent's lips traveled just beneath her jaw, from one ear to the other. "You worry too much."

Ha, wasn't that the story of her life?

His teeth pressed softly into her left earlobe, reminding her that right now, she had every right to worry. And not just about whether or not the man had gone into shock. If he kept kissing and nibbling, she would soon join him.

"But we shouldn't." Kayla stepped back and felt the bathroom countertop dig into her hip.

"Why not?" Brent reached out, grasped a handful of shirt at the small of her back, and pulled her toward him. "I thought we were past all the formalities by now."

Before she had a chance to squirm away again, his lips pressed into hers. The kiss was gentle, nearly a caress. Okay, so maybe he wasn't going into shock. But if that was true, then what was he doing? Surely he knew whatever this thing was between them couldn't work. She refused to lead him on or hurt him like that.

And yet she was unable to resist kissing him back, unable to keep her body from melting into his. It was as if she were a puppet, and Brent controlled all the strings. Heat rolled off his muscular, naked torso, sending shivers racing up and down her body. The clean smell of his body wash permeated the steamy air. Something clean, earthy, and all man.

Desire raced through her like wildfire. By sheer willpower Kayla managed to break their kiss, before things got out of control. Before she truly couldn't say no.

"This isn't about formalities," she said, gasping for breath. "I'm trying to be responsible here. And…realistic."

"Realistic? About what?"

Brent's face was a whisper away from hers, his stormy gray eyes mesmerizing. He nipped her lower lip and when she gasped in surprise, he claimed her mouth once more. His hand left the small of her back and wove into her hair, trapping her lips against his. The kiss lengthened and grew in intensity. He pulled her closer still, and Kayla found herself again starting to cave, to give in to desire.

But desire didn't pay her bills, and neither did Brent. She arched back, straining to put space between them.

"Stop, just stop, all right? You're not thinking clearly. Your life is here, in Mount Pleasant. But mine's back in Indiana."

"No," he said, his face suddenly serious. "You *think* your life is back in Indiana. But what kind of life were you really living?"

Surprise washed over her. "What are you talking about? I have a good life there. I've got my dad, a great job at Wayne—"

"No." He pulled her away from the sink and turned her around so her back was against the opposite wall. Then he planted a hand on either side of her shoulders, boxing her in. "You've fooled yourself into believing that place cares about you. That they appreciate your creativity and your hard work. Well, it's bullshit, Kayla. They're using you. Sucking the life right out of you for their own gain. Can't you see that?"

"No." Kayla felt her temper rise another notch. "No, I'm good at what I do. One of the best. They know that. They value my work."

"But they don't value you."

He leaned forward and kissed her again, less gentle this time. With more authority. Kayla shook her head and broke free from his lips, refusing to give in.

"Yes, they do."

"Oh yeah?" He leaned down so his eyes were level with hers, their steel grays barely containing his sudden, inexplicable fury. "Then why didn't they punish anyone else last Friday?"

She glared at Brent. How many times had she asked herself the same question since that awful meeting in Jacober's office? Self-doubt washed over her anew, but she fought to ignore it.

"I don't know, I'm not them."

"But you *do* know. And yet you still defend them?"

Kayla thumped her fisted hands on the wall of man before her. "They could have fired me, Brent. Kicked me to the curb with a pink slip in hand. Instead, I got a slap on the wrist. They cut me a break because they do value me as an employee."

She stared up at him, willing him to believe her. Willing herself to believe the same thing. But his scowl remained, his eyes dark. Kayla shook her head and sighed. "It doesn't matter, anyway, because I've already pulled together the perfect idea for our next big bid. They'll have to bring me back now so I can help with design and bring it across the finish line."

"Great." Brent withdrew and threw his arms up. "So, you'll go and convince them they can't live without you, and then what, Kayla? Sweep it all under the rug? Pretend it doesn't bother you that they didn't trust you enough to hear you out?"

"Stop it!" She covered her ears. "You don't understand. I'm not a quitter, and I'm not going to leave just because I don't think I was treated fairly!"

"No?" Brent's volume mirrored hers, and he closed the distance between them once more. "Then what would be a good reason to leave? Because I sure as hell think that's a pretty damned good one."

"You don't know anything," she cried, pounding a fist against his chest. Traitorous tears welled in her eyes, spurring on her anger. "You don't know what it's like, being a woman in a man's world. Having to prove yourself all the time." She pounded at him with her other fist. "Trying not to feel. Not to care."

Kayla pounded both fists onto his chest, one then the other. And again. Tears trickled down her cheeks, but still she didn't stop. And he didn't stop her.

Left, right. Left, right. Left, right.

"I don't want to feel. I don't want to care."

But this outburst wasn't just about her career, or Wayne Advertising, or Phillip Jacober. It was also about Kayla facing the collapse of a carefully constructed wall of steel she'd built around her heart. A collapse that had begun the moment she'd collided with Brent Masterson in that silly diner. And despite her best efforts, she'd been unable to stop it.

A sob escaped her as Kayla's arms fell limp at her sides. Instead of turning her away, Brent pulled her in to his red and battered chest. His big, strong arms wrapped around her exhausted frame, and he rested a cheek on the top of her head. "Shh, it's all right. You're all right."

"I thought I'd lost you," she whispered into his chest. "I was so scared you were drowning, and I can't swim, so I paced the shoreline, helpless. And all I kept thinking was how I couldn't save you, just like I couldn't save my mom."

Brent's arms tightened around her.

"But I didn't drown." His voice was quiet as he cupped her chin and lifted her face toward his. "And you never have to lose me, ever, if you do just one thing."

"What's that?"

"Stay."

Chapter Nineteen

B rent watched Kayla's red-rimmed blue eyes widen. "Stay?"

"Yes. Here, in Mount Pleasant." He brushed his thumb along her damp cheekbone.

She sighed, then rested her face against his chest. "If only it were that easy."

"It is that easy."

"No, Brent, it's not. I'm not some carefree kid fresh out of college. I have an apartment. Bills. Responsibilities."

"But those are all things you can walk away from and start over with up here."

"But what about my dad? I can't just leave him there. Alone."

Brent had no answer for that objection. He sighed and kissed the top of her sweet head. Vanilla and lilac flooded his senses, distracting him from his mission to win her heart. Maybe it was time he changed tactics, appeal to her physical side…

His lips moved to the top of her ear. Then just below her ear. She shivered in his arms. Brent could nearly taste victory.

"He's a grown man, Kayla." His lips brushed across her neck as he spoke. "He can—"

A song erupted from somewhere close by. Something upbeat and modern, yet instantly annoying and far too loud for the small bathroom. Kayla disentangled herself from him and reached for the cell phone in her back pocket.

"Sorry, hang on." She glanced at the number on its screen. "Huh, no idea."

With a scowl, she silenced the phone and shoved it back into her pocket.

Brent snagged the belt loops on the front of her jeans and pulled her back to him. "I get the feeling you spend entirely too much time trying to please everyone else."

"I do no—"

She stopped. Listened. After a moment, he heard it too: another man's voice. Only this one sounded very small…

"Oh, crap!" Kayla dug the phone back out. "Hello? Daddy! Yes, sorry, must have hit the wrong button. What's up?"

Speak of the devil.

Brent frowned as Kayla made her way out of the cramped bathroom. Nothing killed the mood like family interference. All he could hope now was that she'd keep it short. Politely excuse herself and come running back to him. He craned his neck to see where she'd gone.

"You're where? He did? Uh-huh. And what did he say? Oh."

So much for keeping it short. With a sigh, Brent walked out into his bedroom as well. He padded over to his dresser barefoot and glanced over at Kayla. Her cheeks were still flushed with what he hoped was desire, but her face had grown serious. Never a good sign with her.

She'd been checking him out in the bathroom, though. Maybe if he could sufficiently distract her, he could get Kayla off the phone and away from thoughts of her father. He gave his towel a small tug and let it fall to the floor. After a brief moment he turned his head her way, nonchalant. Kayla had her back to him, engrossed in the conversation and oblivious to his striptease. She stroked the top of Bear's silky head, her eyes focused on something off in the distance outside his bedroom window.

So much for that idea.

Brent pulled a pair of skivvies from his dresser and stepped into them, then swiped his towel off the floor and traded it for a pair of semi-clean jeans hanging off the back of a chair.

"...I don't know, Dad. I mean, it's not like Joe is going anywhere. Who knows what kind of stunt he might pull next?"

Ah, that's my girl, Brent thought with a satisfied nod. Some of what he'd said to her in the bathroom must have soaked in. He made his way over to his closet and yanked a clean tee off a hanger.

"Yes, I know. I know, Dad. You're right. Yes, maybe I should give him another chance."

Brent tugged the shirt on with a growl. Even without hearing the other side of her conversation, Brent could tell her father was laying it on thick. Couldn't he see how detrimental this guilt trip would be to her in the long run?

"Yeah, I'll wait to hear from him. Yes, he's got my number. Okay, I will. Love you, too."

She hung up and stood there, staring down at her phone. Bear pressed his body closer to hers, eager for her to resume petting him, but all she offered was a halfhearted pat on the head. With a snort, he sunk to the ground.

I feel your pain, buddy. I feel your pain.

Brent cleared his throat. "Everything all right?"

Kayla tucked the cell back into her pocket. "Right as rain," she said, her answer unconvincing as she avoided his gaze. "You warm now?"

"For the most part."

"Good." She started toward him…and kept right on going. "We should probably get some food in you."

Brent stood there, mouth ajar, as her footsteps echoed down the stairway. Damn it, he'd been so close. He snapped his jaw shut and gave himself a mental slap. Now was not the time to give up. She was still here, alone, with him. And she had yet to give him a solid no.

Until she did, it was still game on.

K ayla set the remains of her sandwich down and groaned. "I ate *way* too much."

"Ruby packs like she's feeding an army, always has. I had to choose a career involving manual labor just to burn off the million calories a day she tries to cram down my throat."

Kayla laughed and started to clear the plates from their picnic blanket. She thought they would stay indoors, to keep Brent warm. But he'd come downstairs with an old, mammoth-sized quilt insisting that since Ruby had packed them a picnic then, darn it, that's what they were going to have. Before she'd been able to volley a decent rebuttal, he'd marched out the door. And because outside offered a whole lot more space to put between her body and his, she'd followed.

Now he lay on his back, eyes closed and stretched out like a cat sunning himself beside a window. With Bear inside and a thick wall of woods surrounding the side yard, it was gloriously quiet. Nearly intimate. As if they were the last two people on earth.

Kayla wished she could hit pause on some universal remote and freeze time.

She set their dishes aside and let her gaze drift back to Brent, who looked utterly at peace. The worry lines that typically flanked the corners of his eyes and lips had disappeared. So had the guarded, scowling man who had done his best to keep her at arm's length earlier in the week. He'd been easier to resist, acting like that. But now...

"You're staring at me."

Busted. "Just trying to see if your chest is still moving."

"You really are a terrible liar."

"Whatever." Kayla lay down and stretched out on the blanket as well, careful to leave what seemed like an appropriate distance between them. "You know, when Tommy and I were kids, we'd drag blankets like this out into the backyard and stare up at the clouds for hours, making up stories about the shapes and animals we saw."

"Oh yeah?"

"Mmm hmm. The clouds today would have made for

some great stories." She glanced his way, suddenly self-conscious. "Sorry, I bet that sounds silly. We can go if you need to get back."

"Nah, relax for a bit."

"But aren't you behind schedule?"

Brent snorted. "I haven't had a day off in over a month, so I don't think one afternoon is too much to ask. Besides, it's clouding up. Rain's coming, I can feel it."

"Feel it? Let me guess—in all those manly, broken bones of yours?"

He cracked one eye open and threw her a grin. "Bingo."

Kayla turned toward him and propped herself up on one elbow. "You never did tell me what exactly you broke, or how."

Brent's eye slid shut once more. "Knuckles, mostly. On my right hand."

"Pick a few fights you maybe shouldn't have?" she teased.

"Oh, I didn't start fights, I ended them. Someone had to defend Miles's scrawny ass."

Kayla sucked in a quiet breath. "Miles got picked on as a kid?"

"Yeah," Brent grinned now, his eyes still shut. "Miles wasn't always the tall, handsome chick magnet he thinks he is now. He was a late bloomer, one of the shortest kids in our class up until our sophomore year in high school. You'd think he'd learn to keep his mouth shut, but oh no, not Miles. There were a few bullies who liked to single him out. Only, instead of walking away, the little shit would turn around and taunt them."

"He's lucky you had his back," Kayla said, her voice soft

with awe.

The grin faded from his lips. "Yeah, well, I was there for him, and he's been there for me. It's what friends do."

Friends. The word pricked at her heart. She'd had friends, lots of them, back in high school. Handfuls in college, too, until her mom got sick. Once Kayla assumed the role of caregiver to her mother, there was little time for anything else. College got put on hold for a year, along with her social life. The friends she'd abandoned finished school a year earlier than her. Most had since moved away, all had moved on. Not that she could blame them. The passing of her mother had changed her—stolen her innocence, rearranged her priorities. No one seemed to understand her after that. No one but Tommy.

"So, what do you see?" asked Brent.

"Sorry?"

"Up in the clouds. What do you see?"

Kayla brushed aside her melancholy thoughts and squinted up at the collection of cotton candy clouds overhead. The thick white puffs that hadn't been there this morning drifted lazily between earth and sun, casting giant, intermittent shadows across the Michigan landscape. And with each shadow came what felt like a ten-degree drop in temperature. She snuck a quick peek at Brent as another shadow blanketed them, to make sure he wasn't shivering again. Satisfied he was all right, she looked up once more.

"Well, over there," she said, pointing up and to her left. "That one kind of looks like an elephant. And the smaller one beside it? That sort of looks like a three-legged dog. Maybe the elephant stepped on him in some freak circus accident or something." She grinned at the absurdity of her explanation and wished for a moment that Tommy were there. "So, what do you see?"

"Clouds."

"What?" she laughed.

"Clouds," Brent said. "Just clouds."

"Oh, come on. Use your imagination."

He sighed. "Fine. Well, that one over there," he said, pointing skyward, "kind of looks like the rabbit Bear dragged in a few weeks ago, back when we still had snow on the ground. Only, that rabbit wasn't white anymore. More like—"

"Okay." She pulled his hand back down. "I get it. You can stop explaining now."

His fingers folded over hers, warm and gentle. "Is that what you get to do at your job? Use your imagination to come up with clever advertisements?"

"You know, I never really thought about it like that. But, yeah, that's part of it. There's way more to it than just brainstorming, though." She closed her eyes and pictured a typical day at Wayne Advertising. "I've got to work with our clients, understand who they are, what they want, what they need, who their competition is, what their market edge is. It's more than just daydreaming and doodling, that's for sure."

"It's too bad Ruby doesn't have someone like that to work with. She trusts Miles to figure out all this stuff for her, but he's a numbers guy, not an idea guy."

Kayla thought back to the sketch Miles had shown her. Brent was right—his cousin definitely wasn't a natural when it came to design work. She'd offered some tips, but there was so much more he could do with that ad. Better angles to take, images to add.

Brent's hand twisted inside hers. She glanced over to

find him propped on one elbow staring down at her, the gap between them reduced to mere inches. The sight scattered her thoughts.

"You know," he said. "Mount Pleasant doesn't have an overabundance of ad agencies. If you're as good as you say you are—and I believe you, trust me I do—why not come up here and start your own company? Be your own boss?"

"Brent…"

"Look, I meant what I said inside. You deserve better, Kayla. To be among peers who respect and trust you. And where you can trust them."

Her own company? The thought had never even crossed her mind. Nor should it have—she didn't have the financial backing necessary to run her own business. Or any staff willing to make the move with her. Or clients. No ad agency could survive for long without clients.

"Brent, I appreciate—"

"Wait. Don't. Don't tell me no, or why it won't work." He lowered his face to hers and brushed his lips across her near cheek. "Just…promise you'll think about it, all right? You don't have to go back to Wayne Advertising. Life's too short to settle for less than you deserve." His lips pressed feather-light onto her cheek. Her forehead. Her nose. "Please think about it?"

His honest plea stirred something deep inside her. No one spoke to her heart like that, not in a long time. It made her feel alive. Empowered.

Wanted.

She reached up and ran her fingers through his hair, then pulled his face toward hers. He kissed her, tentative at first. Unsure. But she tugged at his hair, urging him on. Slowly he rolled so that his body covered hers, somehow keeping his full weight off her while wrapping one arm beneath her and the other up through the back of her hair as well.

"Promise you'll think about it," he whispered in between kisses. "Please, Kayla. Promise me."

She reached up and traced the worry lines that had returned to his handsome face. A quiet desperation had replaced his prior calm. Kayla nodded, eager to ease his pain even if it might lead to more of her own. He kissed her then, his previously tentative demeanor gone. The kiss deepened and Brent's body pressed down onto hers. Kayla arched up in response, wanting to be closer to him, needing to be. But was it the right thing to do? Could they truly make this work?

She broke the kiss, gasping for air and searching for reason.

A low groan escaped Brent as his forehead came to rest on her shoulder. "I know," he said, his breathing ragged. "We shouldn't."

But reason wasn't what she needed—Brent was. She clung to him, savored his warmth, his strength. She hadn't meant to fall for him, hadn't meant for any of this to happen. But it had. And she was as helpless to protect her heart now as she was to resist his romantic intentions.

"Yeah." She turned her head and nipped at his earlobe. "But maybe this time we should."

Chapter Twenty

Brent awoke to the sound of a woodpecker drilling into a nearby tree. He had no idea how long he'd been out, or when he'd drifted off, but was happy to find Kayla snuggled into his chest, eyes closed and mouth relaxed. She looked absolutely adorable like that.

Hell, she looked absolutely adorable always.

He lay there, savoring his time with her. Because, like it or not, the chance of her actually sticking around Mount Pleasant was slim. The thought rattled him to his core and drove anxiety like an arrow straight through his chest. If only he could convince her to stay, to give him a chance.

Then again, after all he'd done to her on the picnic blanket after lunch, Brent thought with a grin, his odds may have already improved. He'd taken his time with her, exploring every inch of her body beneath the warm rays of the afternoon sun. Drove her crazy when he refused to give her a quick release. But judging by the way Kayla cried out his name when she finally came, he knew it was all worth it. And as she crested the ridge into ecstasy, he'd quickly followed.

His own orgasm had ranked twelve on a ten-point scale, and he'd collapsed beside her on the blanket, waiting for his vision to return and his heart rate to come back down to earth. Now that it had, he found himself wondering why the hell he'd given up on women—and sex—for so long. He lifted the blanket and snuck a quick peek at the warm, naked body pressed against his.

Hot damn. He lowered the blanket and shifted so as to not disturb her. Not yet, anyway. They had plenty of day left, and the rain clouds had passed them by. He wasn't going to take her back to the inn until he'd employed every tactic he knew to convince her to stay, sexual or otherwise.

The woodpecker started in again, louder this time, and Kayla's lashes fluttered open. He watched as her eyes came into focus on his chest, and then her cheeks turned pink as the realization of her whereabouts set in. But he didn't want her to be embarrassed. Not with him, not ever.

Brent bent to kiss the top of her hair, which smelled of sunshine after basking in it for so long.

Her gaze flickered to his, pink still tinting her soft cheeks. "Hey."

"Hey." He kissed her forehead and savored the way her body felt like silk against him as she turned toward him. What felt even better was that she didn't push him away.

As his lips wandered along her jawline, she laced her fingers through his hair. Definitely a good sign. In one smooth motion, he rolled them both so that she was gently trapped beneath him once more. She sucked in a surprised breath, but still made no move to deny his advances.

Brent smiled against her neck and continued with his lip exploration. Goosebumps rose on her skin as his mouth skimmed across her bare shoulder. Back to her neck. Down toward her left—

"Um, Brent?"

"Hmm?" *Please say you want round two as much as me. Please?*

"I thought you said we were alone out here."

Brent froze. Hearing nothing, he lifted his head and scanned the woods surrounding them. No one there. Confused, he met her gaze. "We are. Why?"

"I think I just heard Ruby."

Blood pounded in his ears. Ruby? Gah, that was the last person he wanted to be thinking about right now. And there was no way she'd be here, no way she would have even known where to find them. He had the Gator, and it was parked around back, out of sight.

He'd just begun to shake his head when he heard Ruby himself. Only it wasn't her in person, it was her on the two-way radio she insisted Brent keep on him while working away from the inn.

"Brent? Brent, are you there?"

"Shit," he muttered, and wiggled reluctantly out from the toasty cocoon he and Kayla shared. "Hang on a minute."

Kayla's brows formed a worried *V* as she watched him pull on his boxer briefs. "Do you think she's checking on us?"

"No." He carefully tugged his jeans up and over a fading erection. "But the last time I didn't answer, she darned near called the National Guard."

Kayla giggled. "Well then, go answer that radio. I'll, um,

just keep your spot warm."

Hot damn.

Brent hurried barefoot around the back of the house and snatched the radio from the hollowed out dash of the Gator. "Whatcha need, Ruby?"

"Oh, Brent! I'm glad you answered. Is everything okay?"

"Yep, everything is fine." Or at least it would be, again, very shortly. He grimaced and squatted to adjust the furniture. Jeans just weren't designed to accommodate hard-ons. "What's up?"

"I need you two to come help us back at the inn."

"What, *now*?" Brent cast a longing glance toward the side yard.

"Yes, you have to come. Mr. Billings's alpacas knocked down another section of fence."

"Okay, no problem. I'll take a look at it in a bit and have it fixed before nightfall." He squirmed in his over-tight jeans again. "First thing in the morning at the latest."

"You don't understand—we don't just need the fence fixed, we need your and Kayla's help rounding the mindless beasts up. The entire herd is in our front yard, eating my daffodils!"

Kayla and Miles handed the last two leads over to a thankful Mr. Billings, then started the trek back to the Checkerberry in what little sunlight was left. Who would have thought those darned alpacas could be so stubborn? They always looked so cute and sweet on television. But after spending the better part of the evening dragging them away from the flower beds she'd spent all week beautifying, well, now she understood why Brent referred to them as beasts.

Brent.

She squinted in his direction and spied him awash in the glow of a portable floodlight, still hard at work mending a broken section of fencing. He'd come back to their picnic spot after talking with Ruby, cursing and apologizing at the same time. Kayla had insisted it was fine, she'd be happy to help any way she could. Though as they finished getting dressed in silence, sexual tension between them simmering, she couldn't help but feel the sting of disappointment.

Why the interruption? Why then, when she'd finally allowed herself to relax? To live a little, as Tommy had said? Would she never be allowed to find happiness and keep it for more than a fleeting moment?

Kayla had promised to consider Brent's suggestion to leave Wayne Advertising—and all of Fort Wayne—behind. After spending the day with the real Brent, the one not hiding behind a mask of grief and bitterness, the idea was tempting. But how could she put her father through that? Of losing her, too? Besides, there'd be no one else to watch over him, to make sure he was taking care of himself. If only there were another way…

"Hey, Miles? Can I ask you something?"

"Sure, shoot."

"Do you think Brent would ever consider moving away from Mount Pleasant?"

"No. At least, not while Ruby is alive and kicking." Miles shot her a curious glance. "Why?"

Kayla shrugged. "I don't know. It just seems like here

he's surrounded by all these reminders of the past. Losing his parents. And Nikki. It's kind of…masochistic."

"To you and me? Yeah. But to Brent?" Miles shook his head. "Me, Ruby, Bear, and that farmhouse are all he's got left. Family was always important to Brent; it came before everything else. He used to get teased by the other football players in college for going steady with Nikki instead of sleeping around like the other guys. They wanted endless one-night stands. Brent wanted a wife, a few kids, and a white picket fence."

"Did all that change when his parents died?"

"No. I mean, sure, the poor guy was devastated. We all were. Ruby lost her son and daughter-in-law, I lost my favorite aunt and uncle. But he and Nikki had been tossing around the idea of tying the knot weeks before the plane crash. She seemed open to it until that fall."

"Did she go back to school or something?"

Even in the waning daylight Kayla could see Miles's features darken.

"No. She was late. With her period. Admitted to Brent that she missed a pill or two."

Kayla could picture it—Nikki panicking. Heck, who wouldn't? Kayla had never had that experience, but a good friend of hers in college had. It was the longest two weeks of her friend's life. Thankfully, it'd been a false alarm. But had the answer been so easy for Brent and Nikki? She swallowed hard and worked to keep her voice steady.

"So, what happened?"

Miles glanced in Brent's direction. "Nikki freaked out. Said she wasn't ready to be a mom and insisted they should 'take care of' the situation. Brent begged her not to end the pregnancy, promised to marry her and be the best husband and father he could be. At first she agreed. The prospect of starting to rebuild his life brought color back to Brent's cheeks, gave him something to actually look forward to. Ruby went with him to go ring shopping and offered to pay for the whole wedding. We were all so damned happy for them.

"But when he got down on one knee and officially proposed, she said she couldn't marry him. Admitted that she'd been seeing someone else behind his back for weeks. Blamed it all on Brent, that she'd needed a break from his depression."

"Oh God," said Kayla.

"Yeah, it was awful. Worst part was, Brent was so desperate not to lose her and the baby that he swore he was willing to overlook her cheating. Said he'd forgive her and put it all behind them. But Nikki still turned him down, said she just didn't love Brent enough to marry him." Miles shook his head, hands balled into fists. "After all he'd been through."

Kayla felt her own anger rise. How could Nikki cheat on Brent like that? Sleeping around with some other guy while Brent was trying to dig his way out of what had to be pure hell?

A new thought stopped her in her tracks. "But wait—what about the baby?"

"After Nikki turned down his proposal, Brent kept trying to reach out to her. Begged her to go through with the pregnancy, offered to raise the child on his own. But she wouldn't budge. As a last resort he went to her parents' house, hoping they could help talk some sense into her. But when he arrived, they said they didn't know about the baby,

Nikki had never told them. Even worse, she was on her way to the airport with the guy she'd hooked up with. They were headed to California, where he was hoping to break into the big time with his band."

Kayla grimaced. "Let me guess—he went after her."

"Yep. Caught them as they were getting ready to pass through security. Needless to say, things didn't go well. The new guy told Brent to take a hike, Brent took a swing at him and busted his lip. Nikki screamed and jumped in between them. Told Brent it was too late, she'd taken care of the situation and to just leave her alone already. Then she and her asshole boyfriend hurried off to catch their plane. And Brent? Well, he went home and buried his head in the sand. For the next eight years."

"Poor Brent."

In that moment, everything became crystal clear. Why Brent had tried so hard to keep her at arm's length, why he'd been so gruff with her at times. They were defense mechanisms, designed to protect his heart. Much like the ones Kayla placed in her own emotional arsenal after her mother died. Ones she wore like a coat of armor still…

"Yep, those were dark times." Miles threw his arm over her shoulders and guided them forward once more. "And then you showed up."

"Me? What did I do?"

"I don't know." He reached over and gave the tag on her shirt collar a small tug. "But by the looks of things, whatever it is? Keep doing it."

Kayla went to tuck her tag back in, then realized why Miles had such an easy time tugging on it—in her haste to get dressed, she'd pulled it on inside out. *Stupid borrowed shirt.* Her cheeks warmed, but she was too distracted by the weight of Miles's words to crumble with embarrassment.

"So this…this change in him over the past few days? You really think I have something to do with it?"

"You have everything to do with it," said Miles, his voice smooth and sure. "So thank you, for bringing my cousin back to life."

They continued on in amicable silence. Miles kept his arm around her shoulder, a gesture that both warded off the chill and made her feel like…well, like family. A family she had somehow stumbled into, one she needed more than she ever could have imagined.

And just like that, Kayla knew what she had to do.

"You get it all fixed there, son?"

Brent wiped an arm across his sweaty forehead then gave Mr. Billings a nod. "Yeah, that should do it. I know I'm not the one who installed the fencing around their pen, but maybe I could come over tomorrow, see how they keep getting loose and find a more permanent fix?"

"I'd sure appreciate that, Brent. Probably make your grandmother happy, too, knowing they won't be knocking down her split rails anymore. The 'pacas, they look innocent, but you know as well as I that they're sneaky buggers." Mr. Billings lifted his John Deere cap and smoothed back what little hair he had left. "Never had all this trouble with the goats."

"Well, you know what they say," said Brent with a shrug. "Never change a winner."

Mr. Billings shook his head. "You just wait till you're married, son. Winner or not, if Mama's not happy, no one is."

Married.

For years he'd blocked the notion of marriage from his mind, had decided to steer clear of it—and women in general—at all costs. But now…

He cast a glance across the Checkerberry's front lawn toward a lone lighted window on its second story. If Kayla stayed, could he truly open his heart to her? Be the man she needed him to be? He'd made the decision to let the cards fall where they may, but was he truly prepared for what came after the flirting, the dating, and whatever else may follow?

Brent wasn't sure. But right now that lone window seemed like a lighthouse to his heart, guiding him home. And for the first time in forever, Brent felt hope.

"I'll try to remember that. Thanks."

"Do extend my apologies when you see your grandmother next, won't you?"

"Actually," Brent said, turning back to him. "I think I'll head up there now. Have a good night, Mr. Billings."

Once he'd gotten his supplies loaded into the Gator, Brent headed for the Checkerberry's big red barn. The thought of seeing Kayla, to be near her again, feel her gentle touch on his aching body, had him unloading his supplies and back up to the inn in no time. He felt a bit guilty for being the dirty mess he was—hell, there was more dried mud visible on him than skin—but this was an inn. There had to be at least a dozen available showers.

He only needed one, and he knew exactly which room it was in.

Unfortunately, Ruby sprang on him the second he

stepped through the back door. "Whoa, there, mister," she said, moving to block his path. "And just where do you think you're going?"

Brent's gaze flashed to the stairs. "Uh, up to take a shower?"

"Oh, no you don't. You're not tracking all that mud and ick in here, no sirree Bob! You have a perfectly fine shower at your own place. Now, out you go."

She shooed him out with a wave of her hand. Brent had no choice but to step back before she plowed him over.

"But, Ruby—"

"No buts, young man. I appreciate all your hard work, but you know better than to come in here like that—even if there is love in the air."

Brent shook his head and stared down at his grandmother. In her seventies or not, the woman was no pushover. Though the scowl on her face looked much less intimidating with that sparkle in her eyes.

"If I go home and clean up, will I be allowed reentry?"

"Brent, dear, you look exhausted. Why don't you get yourself a good night's sleep and start fresh tomorrow, okay? I'll make a big breakfast, and we can eat as a family. It's been ages since we all sat down for breakfast together. And of course Kayla can join us, too."

Panic shot through his heart. He hadn't gotten a full answer out of Kayla. What if her car was ready before he came back? Would she wait to tell him good-bye? Or maybe that she'd decided to stay?

He stared down at Ruby, contemplating charging past her and rushing up to Kayla's room. But as his grandmother put both hands on her hips, he knew better than to push his luck. Besides, she could be the sentry he needed.

"Promise you won't let her leave before I get back?"

"You have my word." She took both his hands in hers, their soft, wrinkled skin so different from Kayla's, and gave his a squeeze. "I'm so proud of you, sweetheart."

"For what?"

"For not giving up on love."

"Well, don't be too proud just yet." His gaze shifted to the lobby and the stairway beyond. "I'm still waiting to see if love has given up on me."

Chapter Twenty-One

Kayla woke the next morning amidst a clutter of note-pads, pencils, and electronic devices. She lifted her head and pried a pen off her cheek as she checked the time. Eight thirty? *Crap.* If she didn't hurry, she'd miss breakfast at nine. Ruby had made a big deal about it when she came up to check on her last night, so it'd be terribly rude to skip out on it. Besides, this was one breakfast she couldn't stand to miss. Not with the surprise she had planned for everyone.

Thanking her lucky stars that she'd thought to shower the night before, Kayla ran to the bathroom to freshen up. What time had she finally dozed off? One? Two? She thought of Brent as she brushed her teeth and hoped he hadn't had to work too late to get those sections of fence mended. After his fall into the ice and all that shivering, she'd been surprised at how much energy he'd had after lunch.

Hopefully, he'll have that much energy at lunchtime again today. A sly smirk stretched across her reflection's lips. Sure, he was behind schedule, but she was here to help, right? And the guy had to take a break and eat sometime. Why not offer him a side of stress relief ala Kayla?

Knowing Brent, he'd bounce back from the physical demands of yesterday. His job revolved around manual labor, didn't it? Too bad she wasn't used to it. Her body ached from head to toe after bending and squatting in those flower beds all week. But hey, no pain, no gain. And a lot stood to be gained from her stay here.

Stay.

Kayla swallowed hard. She'd promised Brent that she would think about his proposal, about leaving Indiana behind. But the decision wasn't a split-second one, and she had yet to convince the logical part of her brain that it was a good idea. Sure, her heart was all for it. As were her girlie parts—oh, Lord, were her girlie parts all for staying—but the going currency in this country wasn't love, it was cash, and his idea of starting her own company was sadly lacking in that area.

If only she could find a way to get him, her father, and her job all in one place, then life might finally be perfect. Well, as perfect as it could be without her mom. That kind of perfect just wasn't meant to be.

She pushed those thoughts aside and yanked her hair into a messy bun. A decision didn't have to be made right this minute—she still had time to think. Besides, until she received final word from her boss, nothing was definitive. Sure, the emails she returned to last night had all been positive, and the proposal drafted so far was shaping up to be top-notch. It just needed her careful touch and a bit more guidance for the designers. But would it be enough to please

Phillip Jacober?

Kayla brushed on what little makeup she had, then grabbed her laptop and headed for the door. It wasn't until she had a hand on the doorknob that she remembered she was still in the oversized T-shirt and cotton shorts she'd borrowed from Tommy's girlfriend. Kayla quickly swapped her PJs for a pair of jeans and a clean, purple tee—right side out—then snatched up her laptop and zipped down the stairs. She hit the landing before realizing she'd forgotten her shoes and socks, too. With an eye roll at her scatterbrained start to the day, she hurried toward the dining room. Shoes could wait, this couldn't.

Brent and Miles sat across from each other at the usual Masterson table, scowling and involved in a low, heated discussion. Neither looked up as she approached, but their conversation ceased when she reached the table.

"Morning, guys."

Miles offered her a warm, practiced smile. "Morning, Indiana. Sleep well?"

"What sleep I got, yes."

She set her laptop down on a nearby table and came around to place a hand on Brent's shoulder. His hand came up to cover hers.

"Morning." He offered her a smile that didn't quite reach his eyes.

Before she could ask what was going on, Ruby burst through the door with a steaming casserole dish in hand.

"Good morning, dear. You're just in time."

"Can I help you with anything, Ruby?"

"No. Sit, sit. What would you like to drink?"

"Coffee would be great. And maybe a small glass of

orange juice?"

"Of course." Ruby set down the dish and looked from grandson to grandson. A look of annoyance skittered across her features. "Brent, would you be so kind as to get those for Kayla? I need to rest."

He threw a warning look at Miles, who gave him a flat look in return. "Sure, Ruby."

"There'll be no fighting at my breakfast table," she said once he was out of earshot.

"Then I may as well leave," muttered Miles.

"You will stay right there, young man."

Kayla looked between them. "What's going on?"

"The boys are just bickering this morning is all, dear. Hungry?"

Worry knotted Kayla's stomach. She'd hoped to bring excitement and inspiration to the table this morning, but at this rate, would anyone even be receptive to her ideas? "Um, yes. A little."

Brent returned with her drinks, and the familiar scent of his aftershave soothed her nerves as he took the seat beside her. She longed to touch him, to smooth the frown from his face, but it didn't seem right, here at the table. After breakfast, she'd get him alone and ask. Though, who knew? Maybe her little impromptu presentation would cheer him up before then.

Ruby served them each a heaping plate full of what she called "Hash Brown Surprise" then took her seat across from Kayla.

"It smells wonderful, Ruby. Thank you."

"So." Miles pointed his fork in the direction of her laptop. "You gonna share a funny YouTube video with us this morning or something?"

She laughed. "Nope, something even better. Only, no laughing allowed."

Brent met her gaze, his curiosity finally peaked. "Oh, yeah?"

"Yep. But everyone needs to clear their plates first. I need fully fueled minds for what I'm about to show you."

A smile stretched across his kissable lips, and her heart did a ridiculous little flip-flop. How had she gotten so lucky to have crossed paths with a man like him?

"Well, if you two would stop making googly eyes at each other, we'd all finish a little faster," Miles teased.

"Hush, Miles," said Ruby, a grin on her face as well.

Ah, much better. This was the kind of mood Kayla wanted everyone to be in when she unveiled the fruits of last night's labor: a proposed advertising master plan for the Checkerberry Inn. Conversation remained light, and plates were soon emptied. Miles set down his fork with a groan, thanked Ruby for yet another fabulous meal, and then turned his eyes toward Kayla.

"All right, the suspense is killing me. Show us what you got."

"Well, after all the fresh air and exercise I've gotten here this week," she started with a smile. Miles half coughed, half laughed into his hand, Brent's face turned beet red, and Ruby just smiled, oblivious to the reference. "I got to think-ing—the inn's occupancy rates have been slipping the past few years, right? But I couldn't understand why. Everything about this place is amazing. So what caused it? The recession, an increase in competition, facilities becoming outdated?

"Well, last night I did a little research. Yes, the recession impacted this area, but the Michigan hotel industry actually saw an increase in customers over the past three years, not a decrease."

Miles shifted in his seat. "Uh, Kayla, that's great and all, but—"

"Shh, Miles," said Ruby. "Let her finish."

Kayla winked at Ruby and reached around to retrieve her laptop. "So I dug a little deeper, and pulled up the websites of every bed-and-breakfast-type business I could find in central and lower Michigan. Then I did a comparison of their locations to here, amenities they offered, nearby attractions, etcetera, with what the Checkerberry has to offer. And you know what I found?"

"What?" Ruby asked.

"That you actually have one of the best locations in the region when it comes to nearby attractions: golfing, the casino, museums, antique shops. Now, you're rather landlocked, but there are other niches out there besides lakefront accommodations. And your beautiful building is leaps and bounds nicer looking and better equipped than many of your competitors, too. Where you're lacking is your website."

"Our website?" Ruby blinked. "But Miles set that up several years ago."

"Yes, but just having a website isn't enough. You've got to keep it up-to-date, list events, post pictures, capitalize on SEO."

Ruby blinked and blinked again. "SEO?"

"Search engine optimization. Look, travelers want the world at their fingertips. They don't want to have to spend time digging around for places to stay or things to do— they're too busy for that. So they go online and do a search for "places to stay in central Michigan." Right now, you guys come up on page five. No one is going to stick around through five pages of search results, not when the casino and brand-name hotels show up on page one."

Kayla clicked to demonstrate. This morning, the inn had slipped to the bottom of page five.

"Can we fix that?"

"Yep. Give me your password, and I'll have you bumped up in no time. I can update the site while I'm in there, too, if you don't need me outside today."

Miles looked across at Brent. "I told you she was good."

"Good enough that Ruby can turn down the offer?"

"Offer?" Kayla frowned. "What offer?"

"Home Depot made an offer on our land, dear," said Ruby.

Miles nodded. "A very generous offer."

"But you heard Kayla—if we update the website, we might be able to bring more guests back to the inn. Right?" Brent met her gaze, hope in his eyes.

She swallowed hard. It was one thing to come up with a master plan or a proposal. But that was where her expertise ended. Come up with a plan, hand it off to the client, and move on. Not all plans came to fruition, which never concerned her before. But this was Brent and his family's livelihood—could she really sit here and promise them that her plan would work?

"Well, yes, theoretically."

"Theoretically?" Miles's brows rose. "Theoretically doesn't pay the bills, Kayla."

"True. But the website improvements aren't the only suggestion I have."

Miles crossed his arms. Brent shot him a dirty look, then

reached out to touch Kayla's arm. "Go on."

"Well, for one, you could consider opening the dining room up to non-guests. Turn it into a mini restaurant. Your food and beverage costs would go up, but with the right pricing points and enough diners, you could easily turn that into a profit."

Brent nodded. "Maddie is one hell of a cook."

"But she's one person. We bring in too many people and then we'll just have to hire in more staff to help," said Miles.

"Or you guys could help on busy nights, until you see how steady the crowd gets." Kayla received two male scowls for that idea. "What? This place would have the hottest waiters in town."

Miles grinned. Brent's scowl deepened. "What else?"

"The off-season. You're sitting on a virtual gold mine all winter long. Why not rent out the facilities for special events? Weddings, business parties—you name it. Maybe even continue to rent out rooms. Just because there's snow on the ground doesn't mean you have to close up shop. People need to get away no matter the season."

"No." It was Miles who spoke. "Ruby needs a break. We can't expect her to run the place year-round at her age. Open season is hard enough on her as it is."

Ruby offered him a weak smile. "Now, Miles. We need to consider all our options if we are going to keep the inn open."

"At what cost?" He pushed back from the table and rose to his feet. "These ideas are well and good, but they also mean more work for all of us. What happens if you get sick, or Brent gets hurt? We don't have the finances to hire people to fill in."

"But if we bring more guests in, we would," said Ruby.

Miles ran a hand through his hair. "This place is like a never-ending hamster wheel. We just keep going round and round and will never be able to get off to go another direction."

"It doesn't sound like you're talking about Ruby anymore," growled Brent.

"Because maybe it's not only Ruby who needs to think this through. What if I'm not here, huh? Then who's gonna be around to watch over Ruby while you're out playing with fence posts? Kayla?"

All eyes at the table shifted to her. Kayla remained mute, her gaze sweeping one at a time to each of theirs. They had become like a second family to her this past week, but could she really leave everything behind to assume such a role?

Was that even what she wanted?

Chapter Twenty-Two

Brent looked to Kayla and saw the surprise in her eyes. Damn it, he'd spent all day yesterday easing her into the idea of staying in Mount Pleasant. Now Miles was throwing it at her like he was a pitcher for the Yankees…and she was a catcher with no mitt.

"Would have been nice if you'd mentioned your desire to bail on us before," he said to Miles. "Or is that why you've been courting this offer? It'd be a convenient end to your career here at the inn, wouldn't it? Ruby gets to retire, you get to cut ties."

"I could give a shit about the offer, and you know it. My primary concern is Ruby and her health."

"Right, because you—"

"Boys." Ruby's stern voice brought silence to the room. "I need to digest all of this. The offer and Kayla's ideas both. Thank you, dear, for all your hard work. Until then, I don't want any more bickering. Offer aside, we have an inn to open in just over a week. I'll ask that we stay on schedule with our preparations." She pushed back from the table and rose slowly to her feet. "Now, if you'll excuse me, I need some time alone."

With that, she shuffled from the room.

"Happy now?" Brent asked.

Miles's eyes narrowed, but he said nothing.

"Brent." Kayla put her hand on his arm. "Why don't you get started outside and come see me at lunch? I can help Miles clear the breakfast table."

The look in her eyes begged him not to pick a fight with Miles. For her sake, he'd comply. That didn't mean he had to like it. He pushed back from the table and made to leave.

Music erupted from a cell phone nearby. Kayla shifted to retrieve it from her jeans pocket, then froze as she took in the number displayed.

"Kayla?"

Her gaze met his. "I, uh, need to take this."

With that, she rose and hurried from the room, taking her phone and conversation with her.

Work. It had to be work calling.

Brent felt his heart lodge in his throat. Would they offer her recompense? Beg her to come back?

Would she go?

"Good luck," whispered Miles as he collected plates from the table.

For once, there was zero sarcasm in his cousin's voice. Brent almost felt badly about snapping at him a minute ago. Almost.

"Thanks."

But it wasn't Miles's heart on the line right now, it was

his. He headed outside to await his fate.

Tommy tossed a wrench into his toolbox, then walked across the shop floor to where Kayla sat perched on a folding chair.

"Okay," he said, hands on hips. "What gives?"

"Huh?" Kayla asked, unable to meet his eyes. She was unable to do much of anything, actually, numb as she was.

A promotion. They'd offered her a promotion.

"Seriously, Kay, you're starting to freak me out. You've been nagging me all week about getting your car fixed, and now that I'm finally working on it, you're being all"—he waved his hands at her—"this."

"Oh." She tried to offer him a smile, even a small one, but the expression wouldn't come. How could it, when her heart was teetering on a precipice? "Sorry. I stayed up late last night. Really late. Working on a new project."

Tommy squatted down before her, his eyes wary. "Is someone at the inn giving you a hard time?"

She barked out a laugh. "No. No, nothing like that. Though I sort of threw fuel on a family feud at breakfast."

"Why's that?"

Kayla took in the worried look on her brother's brow. Thank goodness for Tommy. If he hadn't agreed to come and get her, she'd be back in her suite climbing the walls. Or trying to track down Brent, who was working in the far reaches of the property this morning. And she wasn't ready to face him, not yet.

God, he was going to hate her.

"It doesn't matter." She pushed up off the chair she'd slumped into upon her arrival and stretched. "So, can I see the part you just took off?"

Tommy studied her for another moment, then stood with a nod and led her over to a sheet of deformed metal. Instantly, his brotherly side shut off and the mechanic in him took over. It was the perfect distraction to an abysmal situation. Or at least, it would have been, if she'd been able to focus on what he was saying. Instead, her mind kept going back to the phone conversation with her boss.

"Kayla."

Her gaze shot to Tommy's. "What? I'm listening."

"I just told you the sky was pink and you said, 'uh-huh'. Now what is going on?"

Oops, busted. "I..." Kayla shook her head. She simply didn't have the energy to dodge any more questions. "I think I fell in love."

"With Brent?"

She nodded, then wandered back over to the chair she'd vacated. With a sigh, she sank down and tried to pull herself together. Just hearing his name was like taking a white-hot poker straight to her heart.

"So, what's the problem?" her brother asked.

"It's a long story."

Tommy pulled up a chair and sat down, facing her. "And I don't have a class until two. So spill."

Kayla scowled at him but could tell by the look on his face he wasn't going to let it go. So she took a deep breath, braced herself for the pain, and told him everything. The first time she met Brent, there, in the diner. Him saving her from that long, brutal walk in the ice storm. Their night together.

His disappearance the next day and standoffish behavior the days following. Him comforting her when she had the meltdown by the daffodils. The pond. The bees. The recovery.

The happiness.

"I got back to my room last night, and for the first time in forever I felt sure of what I wanted. What I needed to do. He helped me see how miserable I really have been at Wayne. How I've been under this grand illusion about my future there and how convinced I was that they see me as just another employee."

"I've been thinking that for years," he said. "But you always seemed so excited about that place. I didn't want to burst your bubble."

"Well, he spared you from having to do that. Only, when Jacober called earlier, he didn't talk down to me. I'd never heard him sound so excited, Tommy. My plan and hard work after-hours paid off this time." She smirked. "I finally hear the words from my boss that I've been dying to hear, and now I'm miserable. Go figure."

"Sounds like your head and your heart are misaligned."

Kayla shook her head. "Always with the mechanic speak."

"I'm serious, Kay. Maybe it's time for a change. What did Brent say when you told him about Jacober's offer?"

"I didn't. He was outside when I came back downstairs. So I called you."

"Well, my advice? Talk to him before you make a final decision. Once you know exactly how he feels, you can weigh your options."

"It's not that easy, Tommy. This isn't just about work— what about dad?"

"What about him?"

"Who's going to look out for him? Make sure he's taking his medications, taking care of the house? The yard?"

"Kay, listen to me. Dad will be fine. I'm sorry I can't exactly go down there and fill your shoes, but maybe those shoes don't need to be filled. Maybe a little time alone will make him see how much living he has left to do."

"But what if it doesn't? What if he gets depressed? Or—"

"He won't—he's smarter than that. And besides, even if he does, he's not your responsibility. Dad has friends, coworkers. They'll watch out for him. It's what friends do."

Kayla stared into his eyes, wanting so badly to buy in to what he was saying, and yet unable to do so. She'd played the role of caregiver for so long now. Letting go wasn't as easy as flipping some imaginary switch. And if something did happen to her father, she would be the one to carry it the rest of her days, not Tommy. "I don't know…"

"Look, why don't you take a break from all this thinking and give me a hand with your car? With the two of us working together, you'll be able to drive yourself back to the inn by lunchtime."

Her gaze drifted to her car. It *would* be nice to have her own car back… "Why, does this kind of repair require a woman's touch or something?"

"No," said Tommy. "It needs a trained monkey. Unfortunately, all I've got handy is you."

Kayla rolled her eyes and stood as well. "Like you'd ever trade me for a monkey."

"Nope, never. Though the monkey would never demand DQ."

"You love our DQ trips just as much as I do, buddy." She jabbed him in the shoulder. "How do you manage to stay so upbeat all the time, anyway?"

"Easy," he said, steering her toward his workbench. "I work with inanimate objects all day. If something ticks me off, I just come in here, grab a wrench, and crank on metal until I feel better."

"Wouldn't a gym membership be a little more…normal?"

Tommy released her and shrugged. "Maybe. But who ever said I was normal?"

Kayla shook her head and sighed. She'd given up on normal herself long ago. Today's drama was living proof of it.

B rent sat in the Gator, trying to keep his heart rate in check. A laser blue Impala sat in the Checkerberry's lot beside his truck and Miles's Camaro. Kayla's Impala, fixed. Which meant she was free to leave any time.

All that was left to be seen now was—would she?

He took a steadying breath, then climbed out of the Gator and headed for the door. No sense in delaying the inevitable. As he stepped inside and was greeted by nothing but silence, Brent knew in his heart what was coming.

She wasn't staying. She'd go back to Indiana and leave him and the inn far behind. Yesterday, he'd been ready to fight to keep her in town. To demand it. But today? Today the weight of defeat had him pinned back, feeling helpless and, once again, alone.

He drew near her room and found the door already open, her gym bag on the bed. His hand felt detached from his body as it rose to knock on the doorframe. Kayla stepped out of the bathroom and offered him a small smile.

"Hey."

Hey. All he got was a "hey." The writing might as well have been scrawled on the walls.

"You said to come see you at lunch."

"Yeah, sorry, I'd hoped to have gotten further on the web updates, but I spent longer at Tommy's than I expected." She swung her arms at her sides and looked around. Anywhere but at him. "I, uh, got my car back."

"I see. Tommy did a nice job."

"Always does."

Brent hated this, hated that she was prepping to let him down easy. Only, there was nothing easy about this for him. He'd rather just rip the damn bandage off and go back to being miserable again.

Because miserable, it seemed, was all he was destined for.

"Brent, I—"

"You're leaving."

The sadness in her gaze said it all. Though why it was there was beyond him. If she was sad, why leave? He held everything in—the anger, the words, his emotions. What good would it do?

"I *have* to go back," she said quietly. When he said nothing, she continued. "I can't leave my dad, I just can't. He's not ready to be on his own, not yet."

"When, Kayla? When will you deem him to be ready?"

Brent hated the way his voice cracked on that last word. Hated even more the look of pity she offered him in response.

"I don't know. Until then, I need to stick around."

"And your boss? That was him on the phone earlier, I'm guessing."

"Yeah. He saw my proposal, said it's the best I've done. Offered me the promotion I've been demanding if I'd come back." She sighed, shook her head. "This totally sucks."

"Why? It's what you've always wanted, right? The perfect job, staying close to your dad—sounds like a win-win for you."

Her eyes shone with fresh tears, and guilt stabbed at Brent's heart. This wasn't how he wanted things to end between them. Then again, if she hated him, at least one of them might heal someday.

"Brent, I—"

"Just go, Kayla. Clearly they need you in Indiana far more than I need you up here."

With that, he turned, headed downstairs and out the door without a single look back. Just like the women he loved always seemed to do to him.

Chapter Twenty-Three

Kayla blinked back a fresh round of tears as she threw her dirty clothes into a leftover shopping bag from her trip out with Tommy on Monday. It felt like a lifetime ago. Emotionally, it was a lifetime ago. She was leaving the Checkerberry a different woman than she'd arrived, had finally been able to open her heart up to someone outside their little family.

Too bad it'd ended with the feeling that her heart had been ripped right out of her chest.

"You really leaving us, Indiana?"

She swiped a hand under each eye before turning to face Miles. "Yeah, I...I really need to get back to work. Big project coming up, and they need my help if we're gonna win this bid."

"That sucks." He frowned. "Well, for us. Good for you, though."

"Yeah." Too bad it didn't feel that way. "Can you do me

a favor?"

"What's that?"

She picked up a note from her bedside table. "When Ruby comes out, can you give her this? It's just a little thank-you note."

"Sure. But I think she'd rather receive it from you."

"I know but I…" She felt her lower lip waiver. "I just can't."

A small sob slipped from Kayla's lips, and Miles walked forward to pull her into his chest.

"Aw, come on, now. Ruby wouldn't want you to leave crying like this."

No, but Brent probably would. "I really messed things up, Miles."

"No you didn't." He rubbed small circles on her back. "In fact, you're the best thing that could have happened to us. Ruby's loved having another female here to keep her company, and you gave us some great ideas for marketing if she does decide to keep the place."

"What about Brent?"

"Oh, don't worry about Brent. He'll uh…well, he'll just go back to being his grouchy old self. That last bit I might have to hold against you. He can be such a bear sometimes."

"Sorry."

"Don't be. Everything will work out the way it should. Always does."

She nodded and pulled back with a sniffle. "Maybe you're right."

"Of course I'm right. I'm the numbers guy, remember? Come on, I'll give you a hand with all this."

They gathered her possessions and Kayla gave her suite

a last once-over. The bed was made, trash emptied, and bathroom tidied—all things a guest shouldn't bother with. But not once had Kayla felt like a guest. This past week she'd been made to feel like a member of the family. A family it tore her up to leave.

She paused only once more on her way out, just long enough to take one last look at the lobby, to memorize its beautiful woodwork. Woodwork that had been lovingly carved by the man she wanted most but who no longer wanted her. Then she stepped outside to her awaiting Impala and said farewell to the Checkerberry Inn.

Brent stared at the tape measure stretched atop a board on the sawhorse before him, trying to remember how long the piece needed to be. He pulled the scrap paper from his back pocket to check his notes. For the fourth time.

Damn it, why couldn't he focus? So what if his heart had been trampled on again? So what if the first woman he'd opened up to in nearly a decade had just chosen a stupid job over him? He was made of tougher stuff than this.

"There you are. Come on, Ruby needs us back at the inn."

Brent looked up, alarmed. "Why?"

"Wants to talk, said she's made her decision."

"About the offer?"

Miles nodded.

Brent shoved the paper back into his pocket. Why bother cutting more boards to update a picnic table down by the pond when it'd likely be bulldozed over soon, anyway?

With Kayla gone, the marketing plan would be useless. And since his grandmother was sharp as a tack, she had to know that as well. She'd be a fool to pass up this offer.

That left Brent to go back to his construction contracting business. Alone. Again.

"She gone?"

"Yeah," Miles said, his voice soft.

He nodded, eyes fixed on the tape measure. "Good."

"Tell me something—when exactly did you become the world's biggest asshole?"

Brent looked up in surprise. "What?"

"You heard me," Miles said.

"Wait—she leaves and *I'm* the asshole?"

"Damn right you are. Did you even ask her to stay?"

"Didn't need to. She'd already made up her mind."

"So you just let her go, didn't try to convince her that you actually wanted her to stay?"

Brent stared at him, incredulous. "Since when do you feel the need to offer relationship advice?"

"Since I saw Kayla bring you back to life!"

His words ricocheted through the old barn. Somewhere overhead, a handful of startled pigeons took flight.

"Look, it may have been your parents who died, but you weren't the only one devastated by it, buddy. We all grieved their loss, all of us. The difference is that Ruby and I, we moved on. We knew Aunt Sue and Uncle Craig would have wanted it that way.

"But not you. No, when that plane went down, it took the old you with it. And I, for one, am sick and tired of waiting for you to get your head out of the goddamn sand and start *living* again."

Brent stood there, frozen with shock. "I haven't been—"

"Yes," Miles cut in. "You have. But you can change that. You can go back to being the Brent Masterson we all know and love."

"No, I can't." Brent turned from him and stared out across the barn floor. "That time in my life, the *old me* as you keep calling it, is gone. I was a fool to think otherwise."

"Bullshit." Miles marched over to stand before him. "You can be whatever you want. Whoever you want. But it's *you* who makes that choice, cousin, not your circumstances. You."

Brent looked into Miles's eyes and felt his heart strain against the iron bars he'd spent the afternoon resurrecting. Bars that had kept him safe for years from more heartache but that he'd foolishly taken down the last few days. And at what cost? His gaze shifted toward the door.

"She's out there, man," said Miles softly. "She needs you."

"No, she doesn't." He turned away from the door, away from Miles. "She's made that perfectly clear."

"Just like you've made it perfectly clear that you don't want her around?" Miles's right brow rose high on his forehead. "If you two would stop butting heads long enough, you might find that you're actually—"

"Perfect for each other," Ruby said, finishing his sentence as she entered the barn.

She paused beside Miles to offer him a peck on the cheek, then walked over to Brent and placed a soft hand on his chest.

"She's confused, dear. Much the same way you are. Both of you have hidden from love for so long that you've forgotten what a blessing it can truly be."

Brent stood there for a moment, grappling with her words. He had hidden from love, had avoided it like the plague for years. From what he knew, Kayla had, too. Was that really what was keeping her from seeing how much she meant to him? How badly he wanted her to stay? Needed her here?

"But what if…?"

"Taking risks is a part of life, Brent." Ruby's voice was soft. "Some are well worth it."

His gaze shifted again to the door.

"Stop thinking so much and go get washed up," his grandmother commanded with a grin. "You've got amends to make and an inn to finish getting ready for this season."

"Yes, ma'am." Brent pulled his spunky grandmother into a bear hug and whispered in her ear, "And thank you. For not giving up on me or the inn."

"I'd never dream of it," she whispered back.

Kayla returned home to a lockbox full of junk mail and a refrigerator full of spoiled food. Well, half full. She'd been due for a trip to the grocery store even before she'd skipped town a week ago. With a sigh, she started to unpack and did her best to block Brent, Ruby, Miles, and the inn from her mind.

And failed miserably.

After being in her silent, lonely apartment for barely an hour, Kayla headed back out the door. Usually after spending three hours in the car, she was cured of wanting to leave home again for a day or two. Not today. No, today a trip to one of their local noisy supermarkets was exactly what she needed. All that chaos might be just enough to drown out her thoughts of the surrogate family she'd left behind. A family who had received her with arms wide open, taken care of her as if she were their own, and yet she'd bailed on them when they probably needed her most.

But it was best this way, she reminded herself as she wove mindlessly through the grocery aisles. A clean break for all of them. Ruby could shop for a quiet retirement villa, Miles could go do whatever it was finance guys do with extra time on their hands, and Brent...

Kayla snagged a cereal box from the nearest shelf. She read every ingredient, every nutrition fact. Cheerios were heart healthy? Huh, who knew? She tossed the box into her cart and gripped the handle tighter than necessary. No more dwelling on the past. Life was too short to live wallowing in regret, and Lord knows she had plenty.

Like her most recent — going off on Phillip Jacober while fighting late afternoon traffic as she passed through Grand Rapids. Yeah, maybe not the best time for him to call and tell her the board had rejected his recommendation to pay her for her time off. On the bright side, her former boss was sure to stop calling now. And since he'd quietly requested she clear out her desk this weekend with no one but the security guard around, she wouldn't have to deal with any departure drama.

At least he'd agreed to pay her six weeks of severance pay, after she'd threatened to sue Wayne Advertising for withholding overtime pay from her for years. Not enough to live off for long, but better than nothing. Maybe her hanging out with a bossy Neanderthal the past week had paid off after all.

A bossy, sexy Neanderthal. Who'd taught her how to feel again, then stolen her heart.

Nope, no regrets, she reminded herself as she headed to the checkout lanes. If she hadn't met Brent, she'd still be under the illusion that Wayne Advertising appreciated and respected her. Both not true. Plus, she never would have met Ruby, or Miles, and rediscovered the importance of family— even if they had their fair share of dysfunction. Didn't most families?

Kayla headed home, consumed by a new dilemma— how to break the news that she'd quit to her father. That was, if Jacober hadn't already blabbed. With her recent bout of bad luck, it wouldn't surprise her. But if she could craft her explanation into something that her father could under- stand, maybe he wouldn't be as worried about her. She had the severance pay, after all, and a terrific résumé that was certain to help her land another job soon enough.

At least, she sure hoped so.

She pulled her car into the lot at her complex and looked for an empty parking space. But all the ones along the front walk to her building were already taken. Lots of sports cars, shiny and new, as if to rub it in. Kayla glared at a red one as she continued past her door.

Oh well, she thought as she slid into a spot in the back row, three doors down. At least it wasn't—

A raindrop hit her windshield. Then another. And another.

She peered up at the darkening clouds in disbelief. "Are you kidding me?"

By the time she parked and climbed out of her Impala,

a gentle spring rain was falling. Gentle, but ice cold. She dug into her trunk, grabbed the bags containing frozen and re-frigerated items, and hurried for her apartment. With clothes already more or less soaked, she set the bags just inside the door and didn't bother hunting for an umbrella. Instead she turned and braced herself for a second tromp out into the great—and wet—outdoors.

Kayla dashed back out into the blinding rain. Several men came running from the parking lot, headed in the op-posite direction. *So much for modern chivalry.*

To her surprise, a man came up beside her and reached into the trunk to help. Usually, she'd be wary of help from a stranger, even in her safe pocket of Fort Wayne. But not today. Today she just wanted to get out of the rain and into some warm, dry clothes.

"Thanks so much," she said, reaching to pull the far bags closer to the edge.

"Anytime, princess."

Kayla stopped in mid stretch. That voice. It couldn't possibly be.

She turned to get a better look at the man peering down into the grocery bag in his hands and gasped. "Brent? W-what are you doing here?"

"Helping you unload groceries, from the look of things." He stood beside her, his rain-soaked T-shirt matted to his muscular torso, looking like some Greek god. As rivulets of water cascaded down his face, a slow smile formed on his lips. "I had no idea you were such a chocoholic."

"I'm not." Mortified, Kayla swiped her shopping bag from him, set it back in the trunk, and shifted to stand be-tween him and her stash. Usually when she went on a pity trip to the store, the reason for her mass intake of chocolate wasn't around to witness it. "There was a sale."

"Uh-huh."

"There was!" Which wasn't a complete lie. "Now, dang it, answer my question."

Confusion clouded his handsome face. "I said I was—"

"*No*. Why. Are. You. Here?"

"You forgot something."

"I did?" The hope spawned by his appearance beside her car faded. "Well, why didn't you just put it in the mail?"

"Because. This item doesn't travel well in the back of a UPS truck."

"Oh?" She couldn't think of anything she'd left behind that might have been too fragile to ship. "What is it?"

Brent cupped a hand to her cheek, then lowered his face to within a whisper of hers. "Me."

He pressed his wet lips softly into hers, and a rush of warmth swept through Kayla's rain-soaked body.

"You told me to go."

He kissed her forehead. "I was an idiot."

"Not gonna argue with that. Though I didn't give you much of a chance to say otherwise."

"No, you didn't. So I had to make a road trip, ask you to reconsider in person."

She grinned up at him. "Ruby made you come, didn't she?"

"She might have smacked some sense into me."

"Smart woman."

"Almost as smart as the one I've fallen in love with." He brushed a thumb across her damp cheek. "Too bad she lives out of state."

Kayla's heart swelled with hope. "She does?"

"Yep. Damn Hoosier."

A grin crept across her face. "Something tells me if you made her a good enough offer, she might be willing to consider it. Maybe even relocate."

"And leave her old job?" he asked.

"Already done. Funny what love can give you the courage to do."

He kissed her then, and the world around them seemed to fall away. Kayla no longer cared about what obstacles might lay ahead with her career or her father. With Brent by her side she felt ready to take on the world.

A car drove through the lot, splashing them with water from a nearby growing puddle. Their kiss ended as both gasped in shock from the icy deluge. Kayla clung to Brent in an attempt to stay warm.

"So," he said. "I guess all she needs now is that good offer, huh?"

"Yep."

"How about we go inside and I share that offer with you?" Brent looked toward her apartment building and back, then arched his right brow. "In great detail."

Kayla gazed up at Brent's handsome face, made even more so by the ornery grin tugging at his lips. Oh yeah, she was in love with this man. He had given so much of himself to her this past week, and she to him. Each had helped the other face their old nightmares, conquer them, and provide the strength to move on.

All of that had been enough to win her over. But any man willing to drive three hours to confess his love to her, and then, once there, do it in the pouring rain? Well, that man definitely deserved a chance at forever.

"Does this offer happen to include a hot shower?" she asked.

"For you, princess," he said, swinging her up into his arms. "Anything."

Epilogue

Kayla stood in her empty living room, giving the space one last glance before heading to the main office and dropping off her keys. She was doing it—she was actually going to leave Indiana behind. While she hadn't been in this particular—and overly pricey—apartment for long, she'd lived in the Fort her whole life. But it was high time she turned over a new leaf.

Even her father had agreed.

"Good grief, woman. Aren't you ready yet?"

She turned to see Brent standing in the foyer, hands on hips and impatience written all over his flushed face. If she'd learned one thing about him these past few weeks, it was that Brent Masterson didn't sit still for long. She'd break him of that, eventually. For now, she didn't mind him keeping her in motion—at the inn, or in their bedroom.

"Be nice, I'm having a moment."

He came to stand behind her and wrapped a pair of

warm, strong arms around her waist. "Sorry," he whispered. "I don't think like a girl."

"We'll work on that."

"No we won't, that's why I have you. So *you* can think like that."

"And you'll just think with your muscles, right?"

His breath washed over her as he pressed a kiss into the hollow beneath her ear. "Or maybe just one."

"I'm trying to be serious here."

"Me too." He nipped at her earlobe. "It's too bad the bed's already loaded. We could have—"

"Don't tell me you two are in here making out again? If this keeps up, we'll never get on the road."

"Shut it, Miles," said Brent.

Kayla grinned. She'd missed having Tommy around these last few years, and the playful banter they used to share. In a few hours, she'd be living in the same town as him once again, along with her new beau and surrogate brother and grandmother. There would be plenty of banter to go around, that was for sure. Hopefully plenty of freelance advertising work to be found as well.

Brent tried to pull back from her, but Kayla hugged his arms against her, savoring the moment.

"You worried about your father?"

Her gaze shifted instinctively to the mantle where a picture of her family used to sit. "A little, but he swore to me he'd be just fine, and that I could call or come back for a visit anytime. Honestly, when I went to visit him last night I got the feeling he couldn't wait for me to leave. Said he was going *out*."

"Oooh, somebody's old man had a date."

Kayla shot Miles a dirty look. "It was with a friend. Who might also have been female."

"Nothing wrong with that." Miles waggled his brows.

"Speaking of which," she asked. "How did yours go last night, lover boy?"

"You know, the usual. Dinner, dancing, came back to my place." He shrugged. "She couldn't get enough of me."

"You keep telling yourself that, buddy," Brent said.

"Be nice." Kayla turned to throw him a look that said the same. "Miles will find love someday, too."

"Oh, no I won't." He shook his head, backing away toward the door. "Love is definitely not in the future for this guy. Thanks, but no thanks."

"Mmm hmm." Kayla watched him disappear out the front door. "We'll see."

"Not if we don't get on the road already." Brent gave her belt loop a gentle tug. "Can we go now?"

"You really don't like being away from the inn, do you?"

"No, it's that I don't like being away so long from you. These past few days without you were brutal."

Kayla grinned. Coming home to pack after spending the two weeks helping with the inn's successful season opening had sucked. Sleeping alone had sucked even more. It was funny how quickly she'd gotten used to sharing a bed with the brawny man before her. "Me too. Though you do realize that long road trips always wear me out."

"Good thing I have a nice, comfy bed at my place." Brent pulled her close and kissed her thoroughly. "We could always go back and rest. Or something."

She stared up at the handsome man before her, still trying to believe that this was all real. That her luck had finally changed. Who would have thought an unexpected detour on a dreadful, icy day could bring her true love?

"Hmm," she said. "How about 'or something' and then we take a nap together?"

Brent grinned. "Now there's an offer I'll never turn down."

Acknowledgments

I'd like to send a big shout-out to my wonderful beta readers Michele, Kelly, Shari, Jen, and Jessica. Your eagerness to read and offer feedback gives me the boost I need to keep writing every time. Thank you also to my beloved KickAss Chicks, who entertained, inspired, and comforted me during my edits and rewrites. To my agent, Dawn, thank you for your excitement about this series and all the hard work you do. Many thanks also to Alycia at Entangled who helped me craft *Detour* into an even more beautiful love story. And last, but not least, thank you to my wonderful, supportive cast of family and friends. I love you all!

About the Author

Kyra Jacobs is an extroverted introvert who writes of love, humor, and mystery in the Midwest and beyond. Her romance novels range from sweet contemporaries to urban suspense, and paranormal/fantasy to YA. No matter the setting, Kyra employs both humor and chaos to help her characters find inspiration and/or redemption on their way to happily ever after.

When the Hoosier native isn't pounding out scenes for her next book, she's likely outside, elbow-deep in snapdragons or spending quality time with her sports-loving family. Kyra also loves to read, tries to golf, and is an avid college football fan.

Be sure to stop by her website www.KyraJacobs. wordpress.com to learn more about her novels and ways to connect with her on social media.

www.ingramcontent.com/pod-product-compliance
Lightning Source LLC
Chambersburg PA
CBHW050410260626
47156CB00003B/947